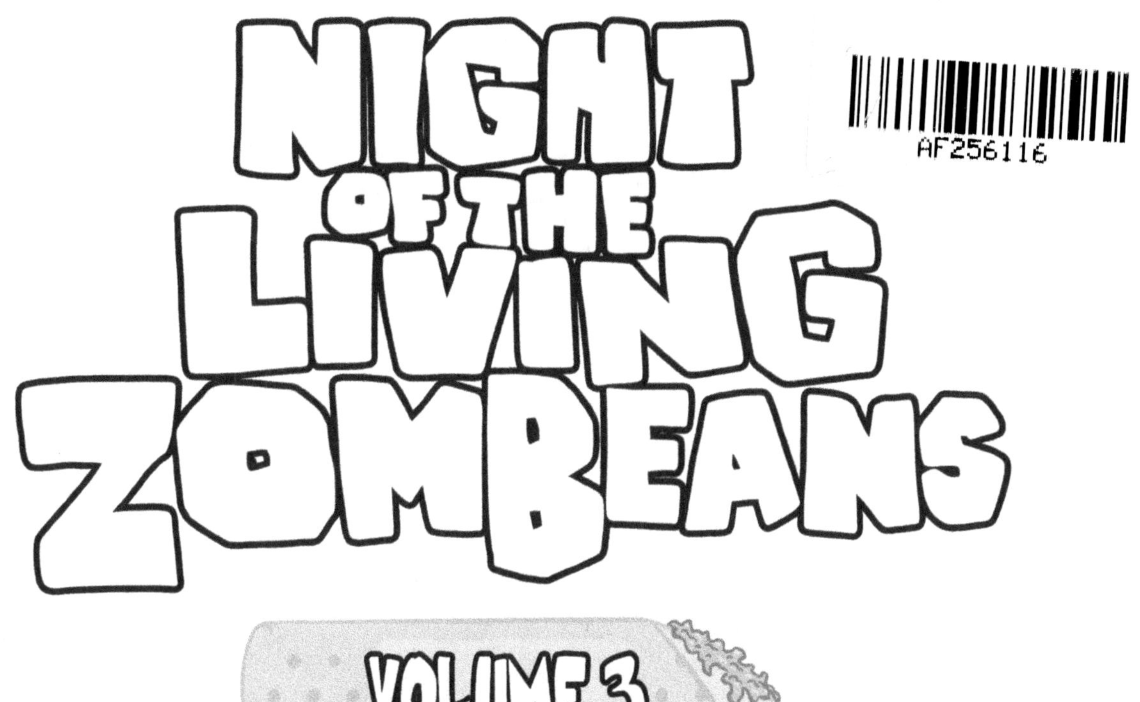

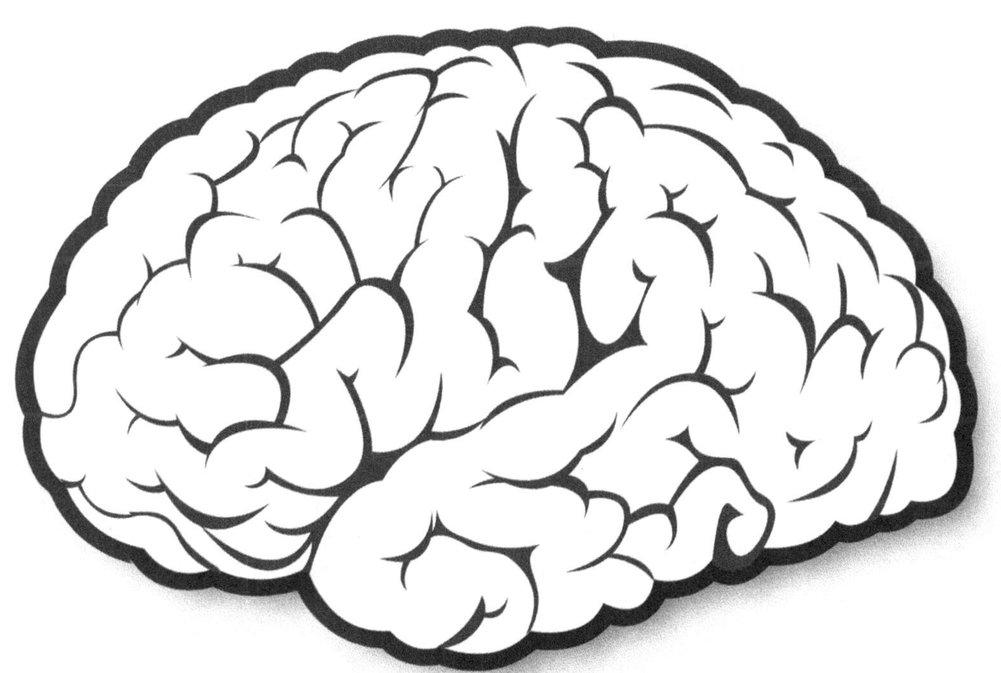

Created by

Donovan Scherer

Born from mad science gone wrong
in the world of Fear & Sunshine,
the ZomBeans have risen
to consume the brains of the living.

SPECIAL THANKS TO EVERYONE WHO HAS
UNDERGONE THE PROCESS OF ZOMBEANIFICATION:

LIZ, MALARI, KARSEN, KAYLA, MARY BETH,
JAYDEN, EMILEE, JEREMY, MEREDITH, JEFFY,
RIVER, KYRA, HYDN, SHARON & ANDY, CRYSTAL,
OLIVIA, MARY, RANDY & LEAH, CHRISSY,
BLAKE, RYAN, AND SHARON

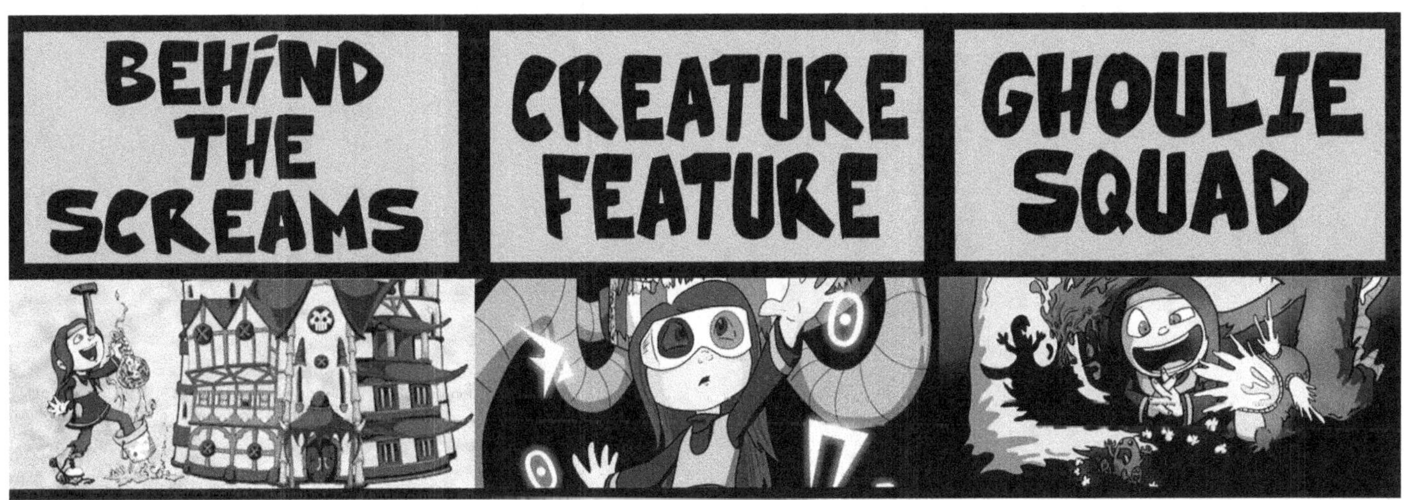

BECOME A ZOMBEAN AT:
WWW.PATREON.COM/DONOVANSCHERER

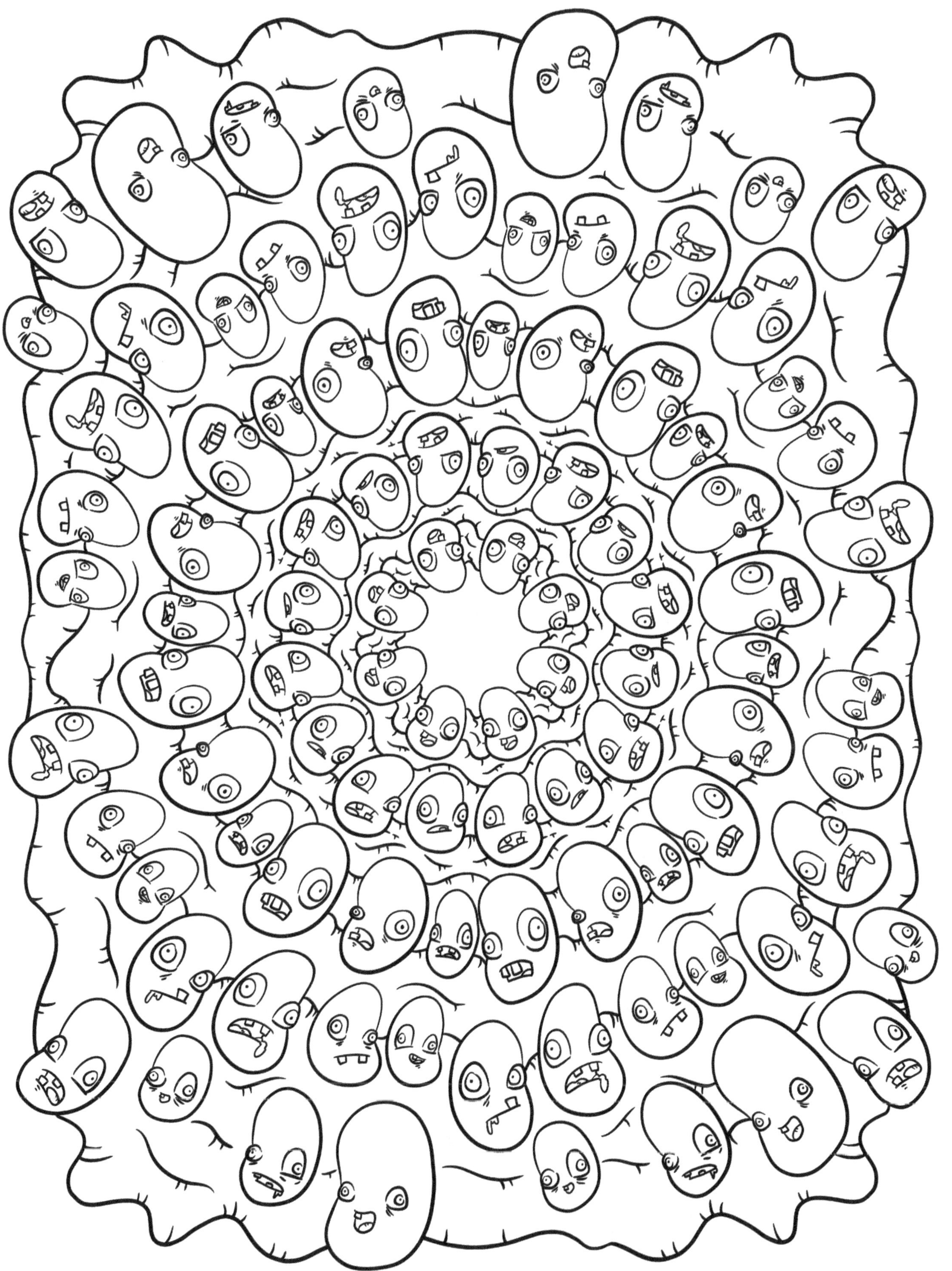

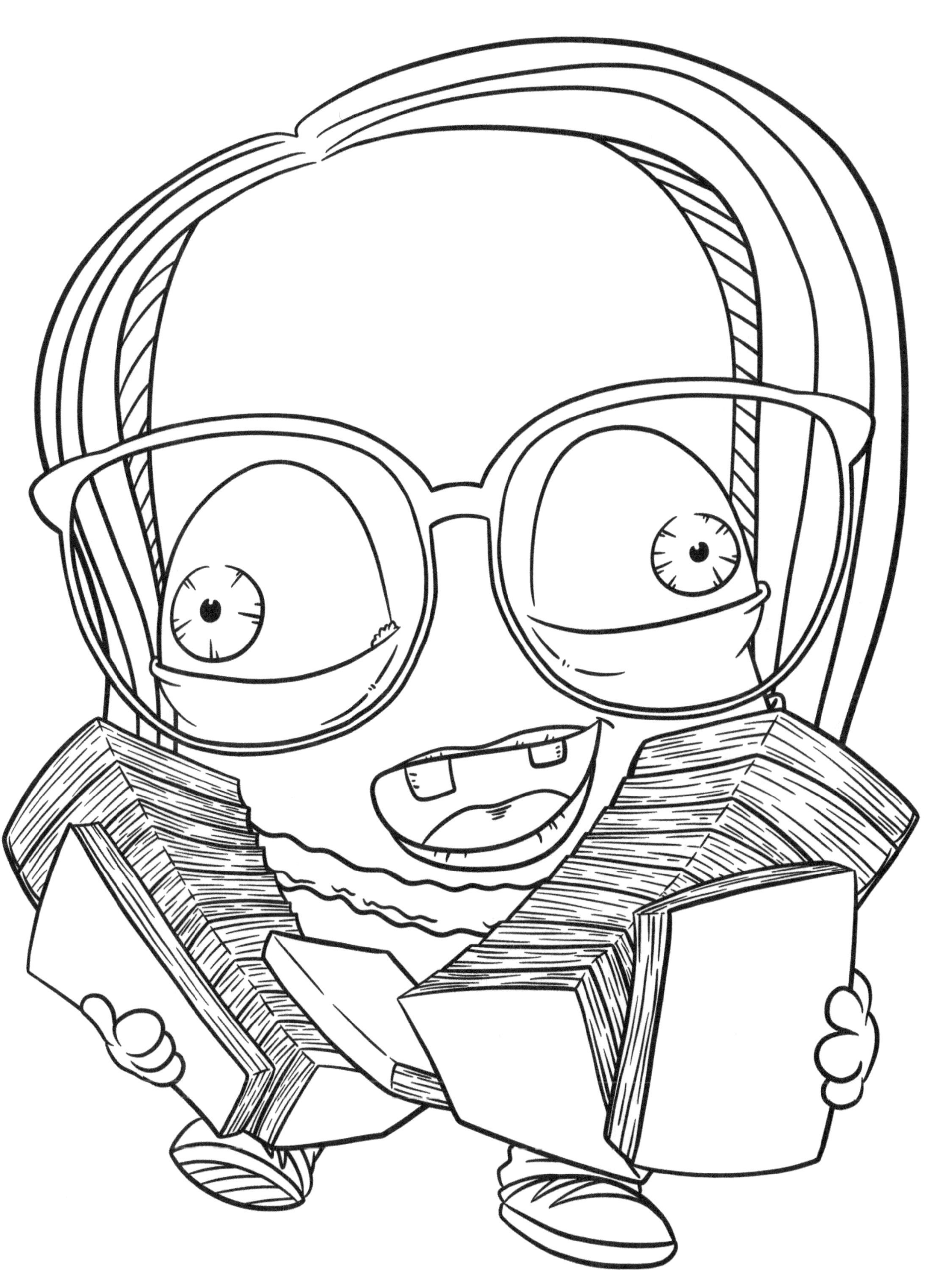

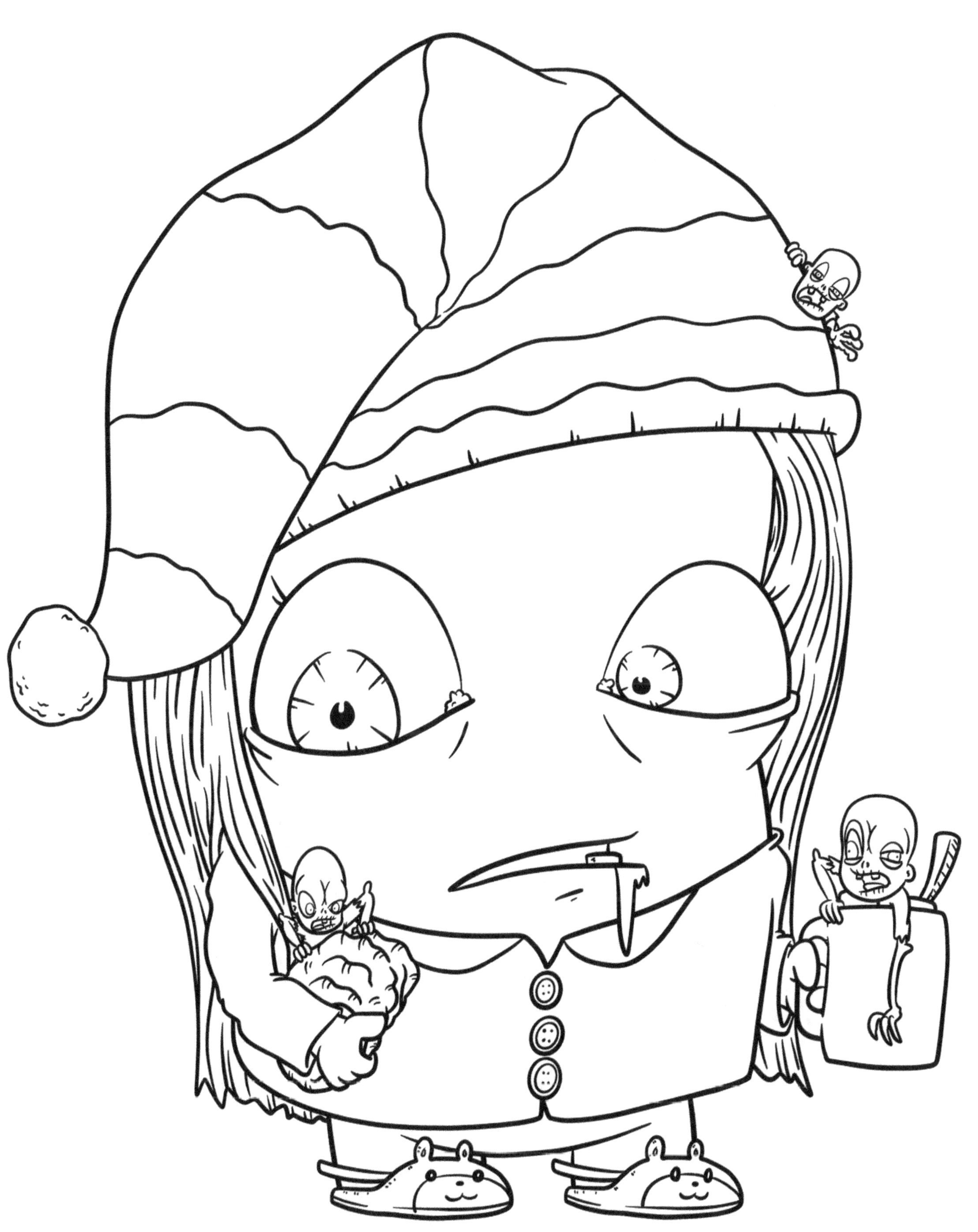

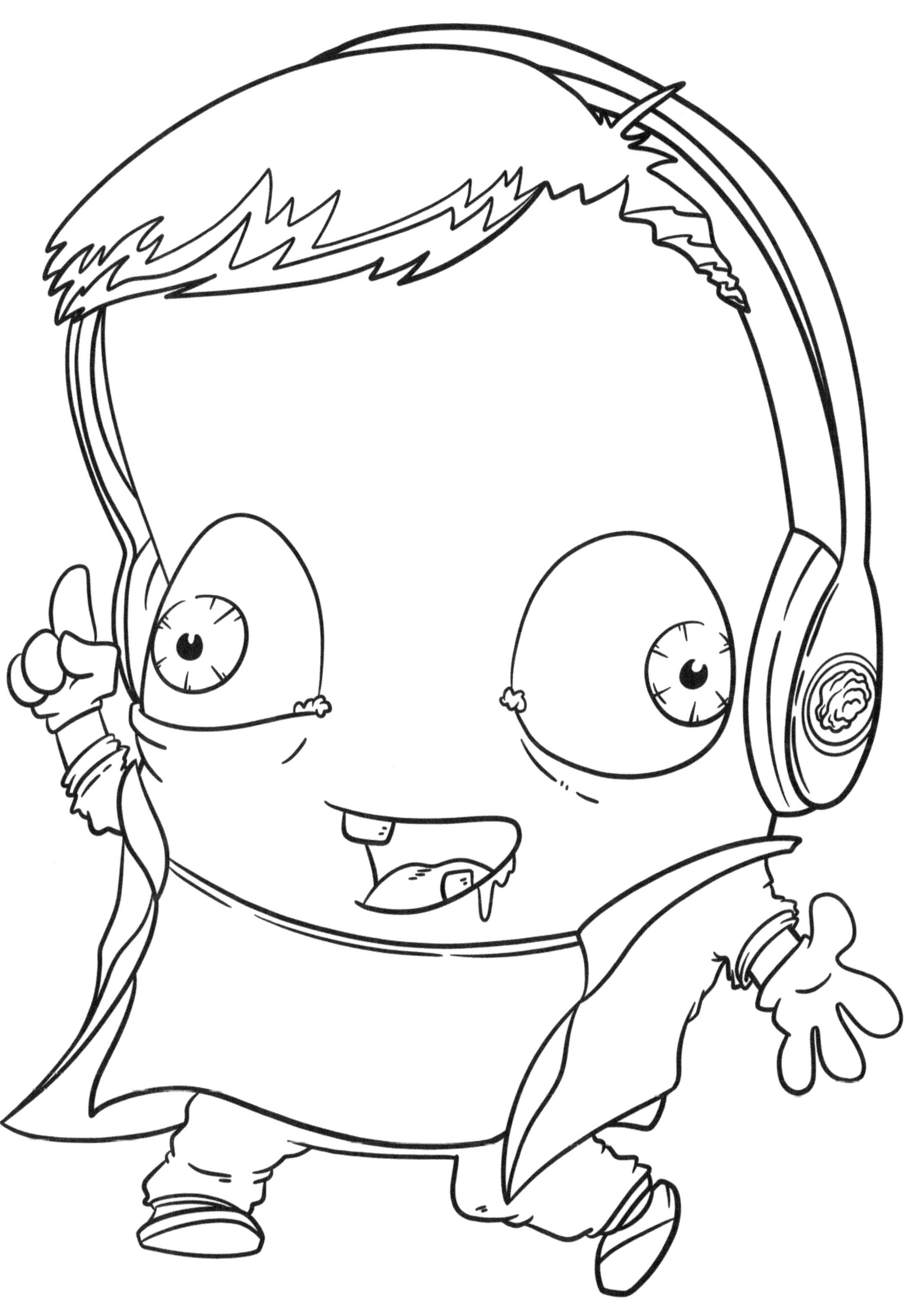

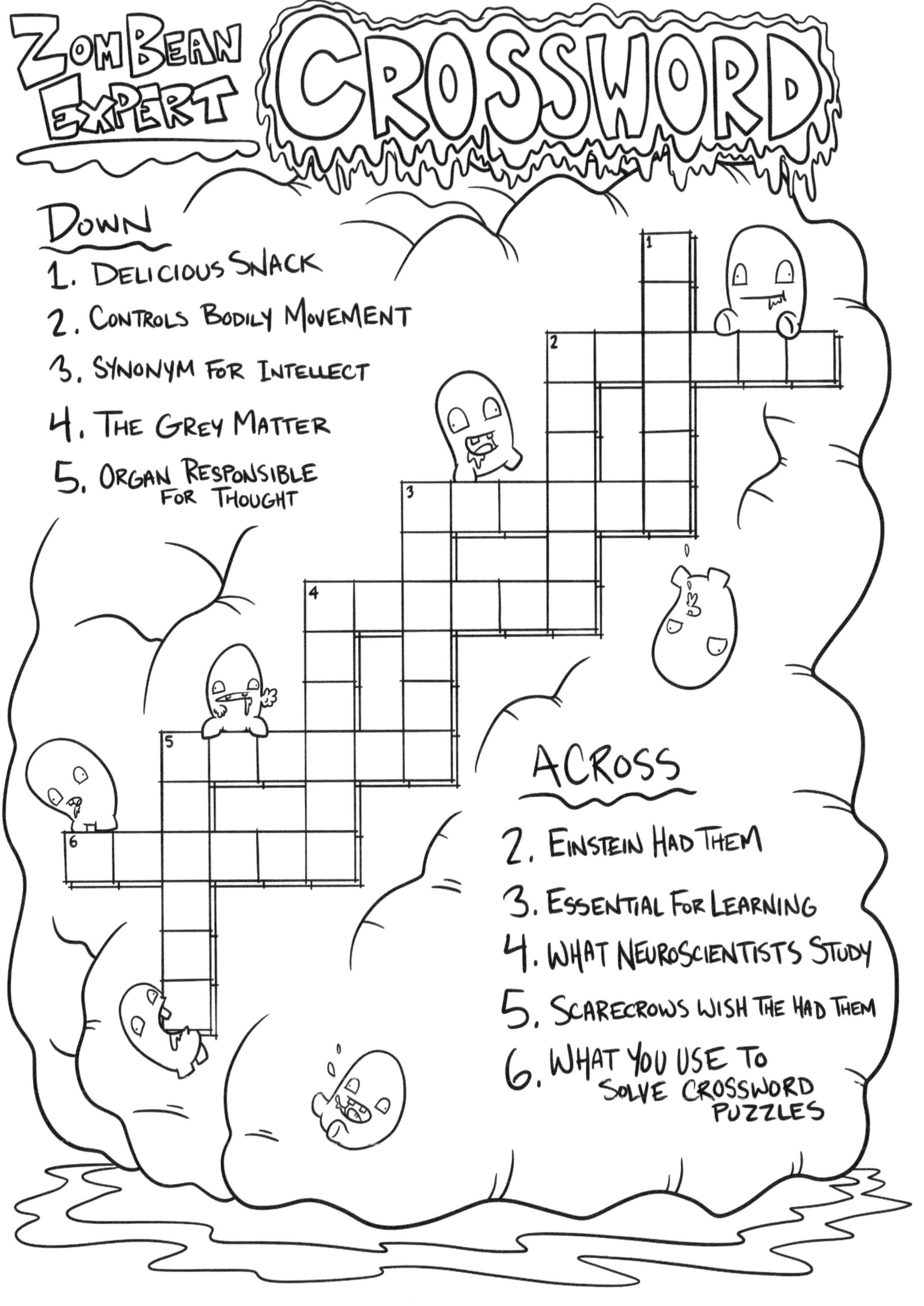

ZomBean Expert CROSSWORD

Down
1. Delicious Snack
2. Controls Bodily Movement
3. Synonym For Intellect
4. The Grey Matter
5. Organ Responsible For Thought

Across
2. Einstein Had Them
3. Essential For Learning
4. What Neuroscientists Study
5. Scarecrows Wish The Had Them
6. What You Use To Solve Crossword Puzzles

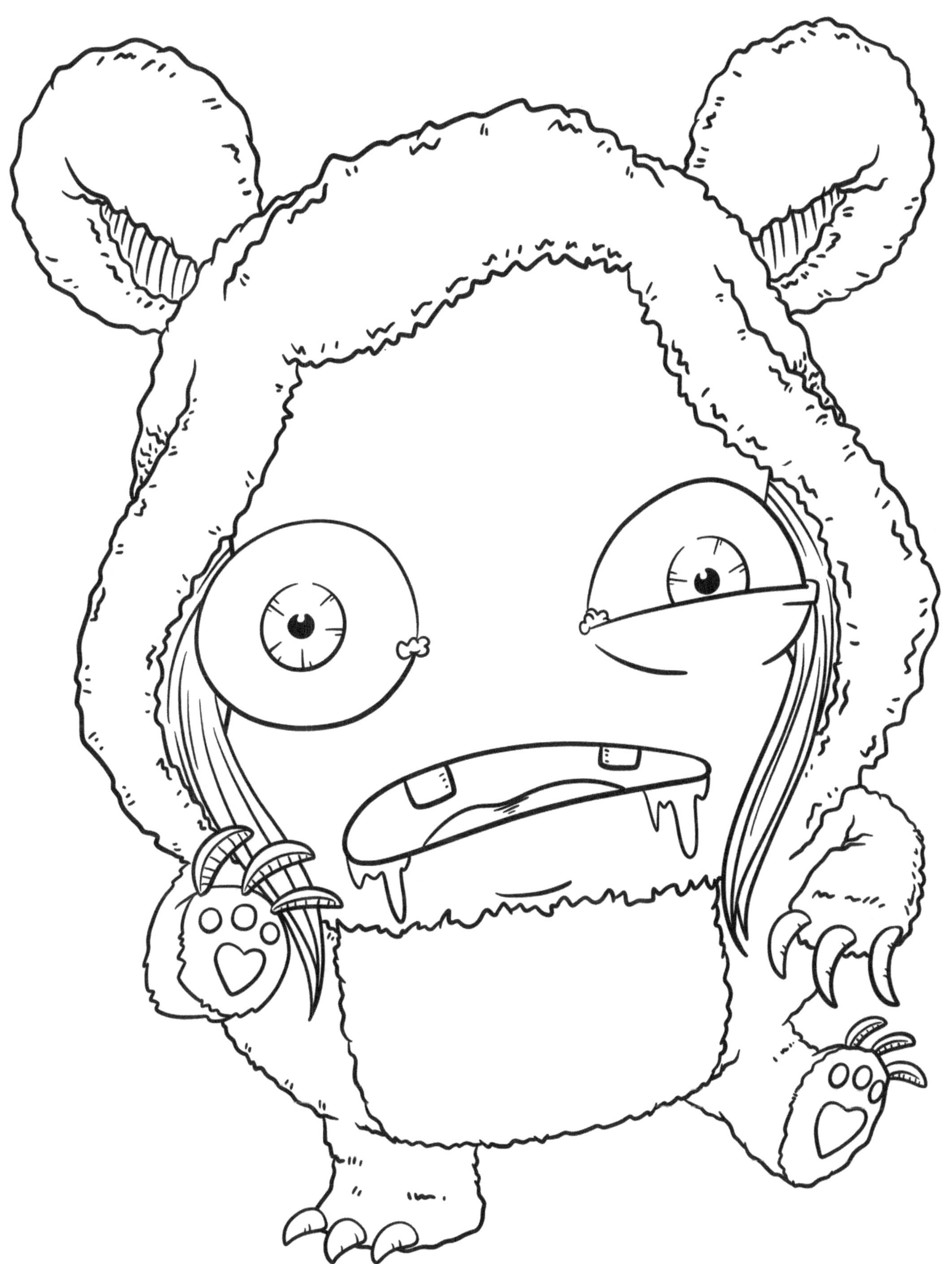

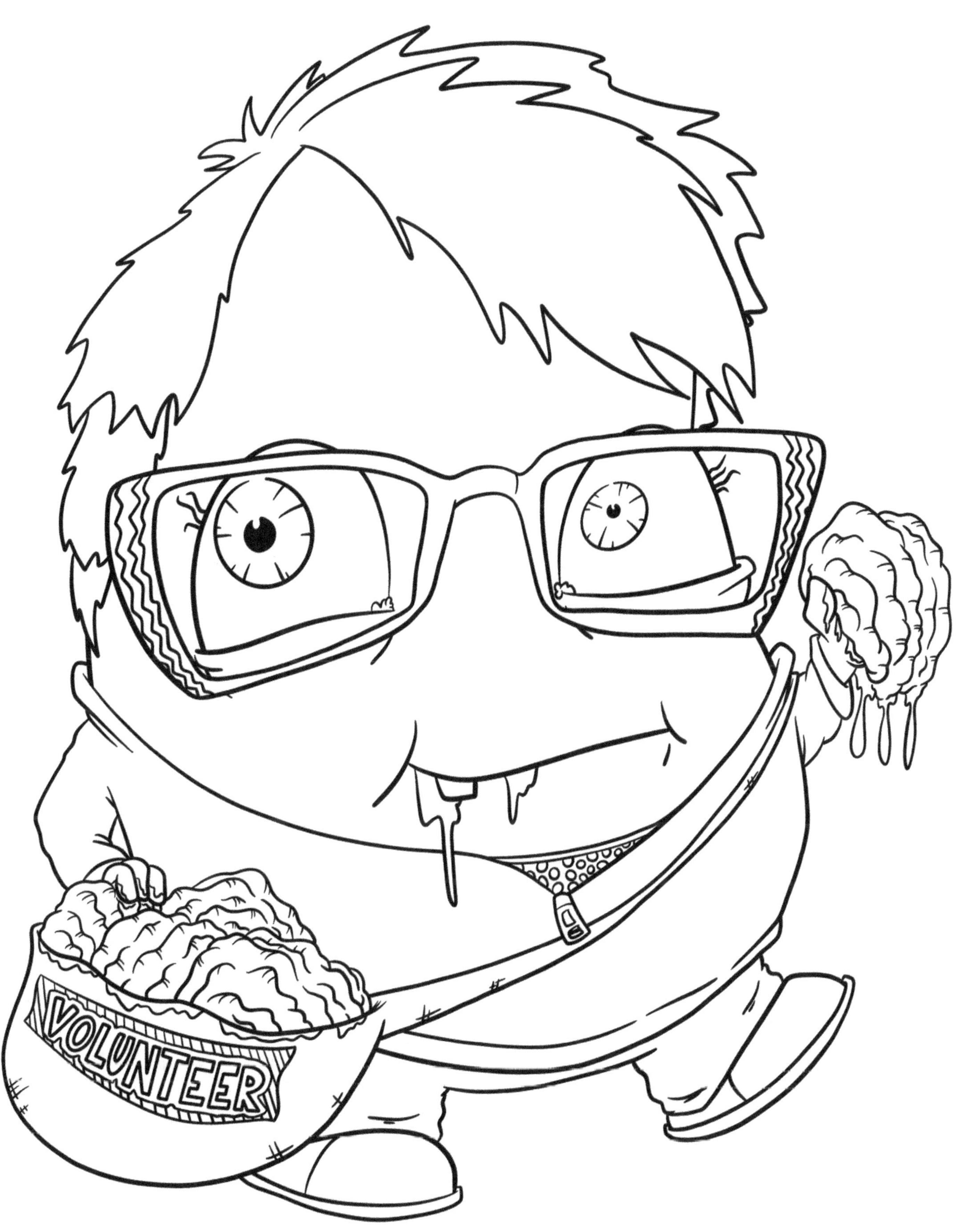

VOLUNTEER

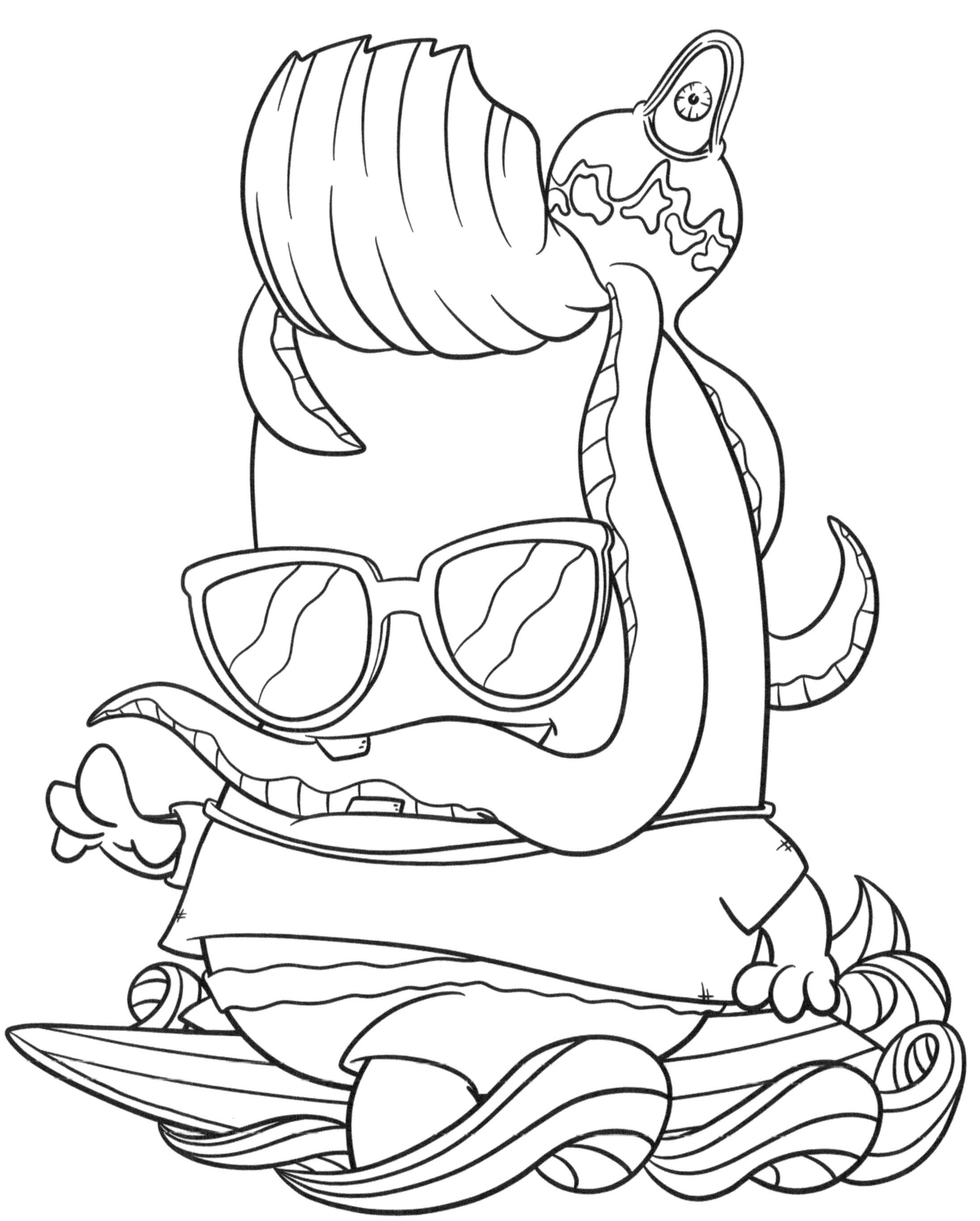

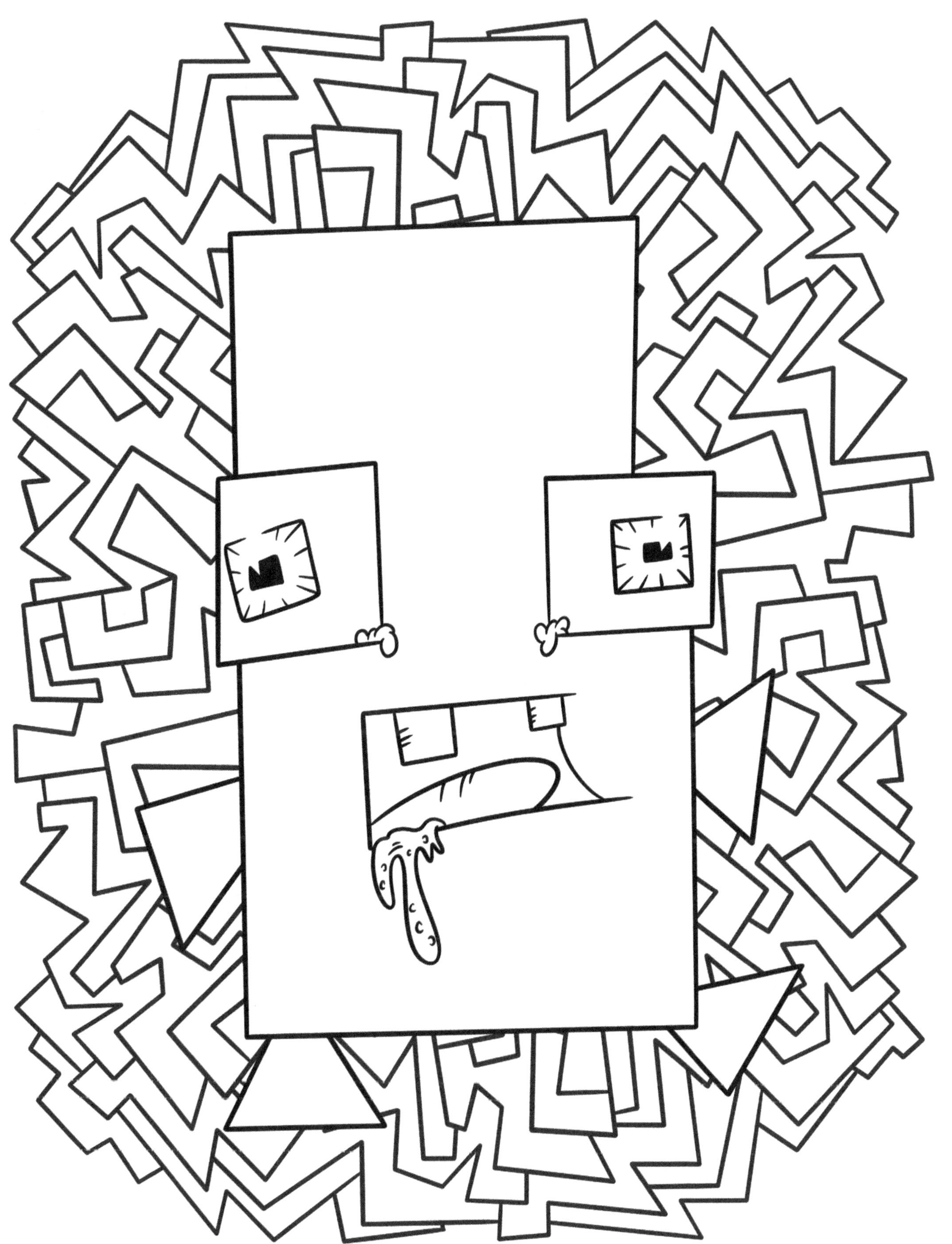

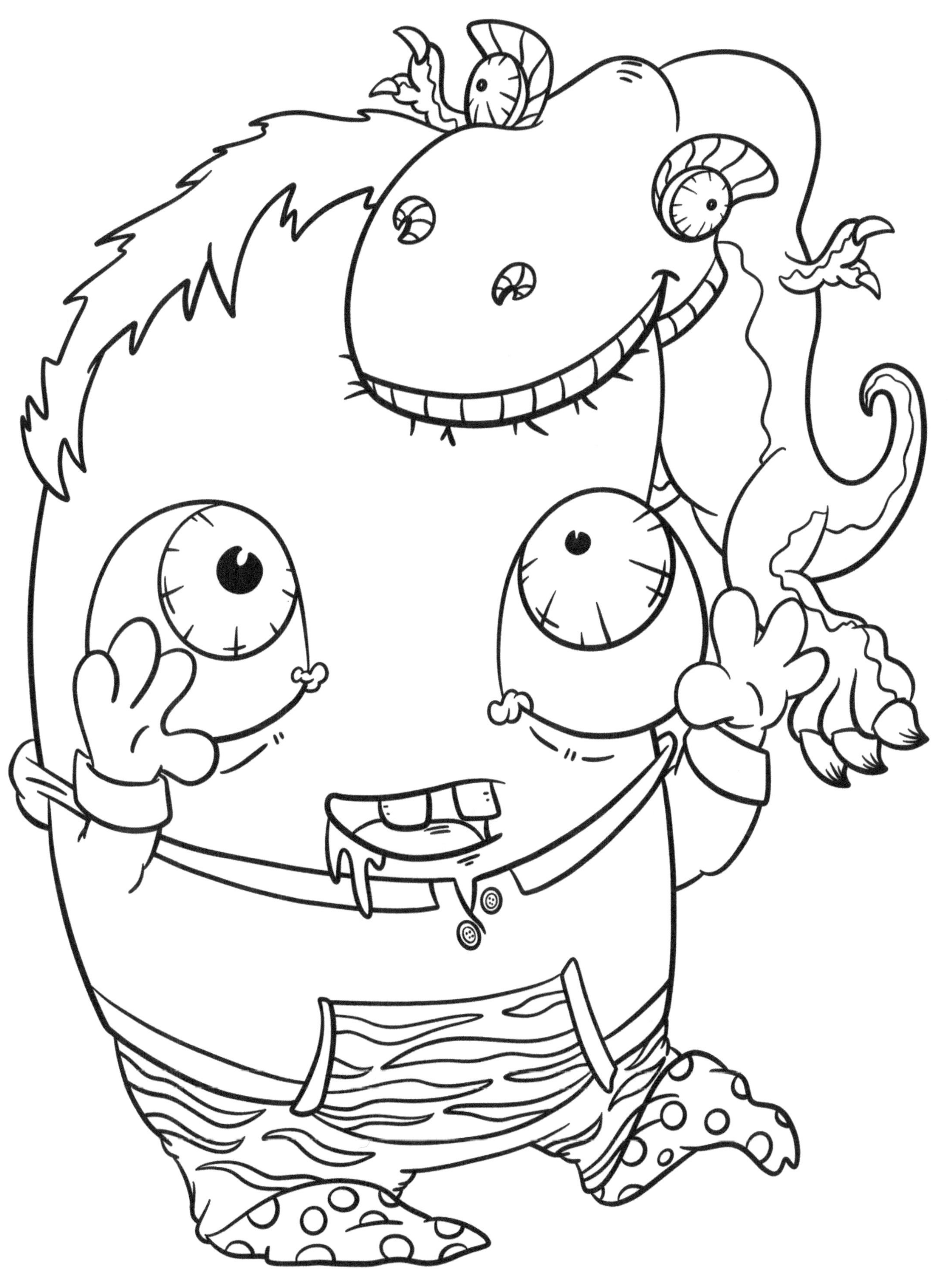

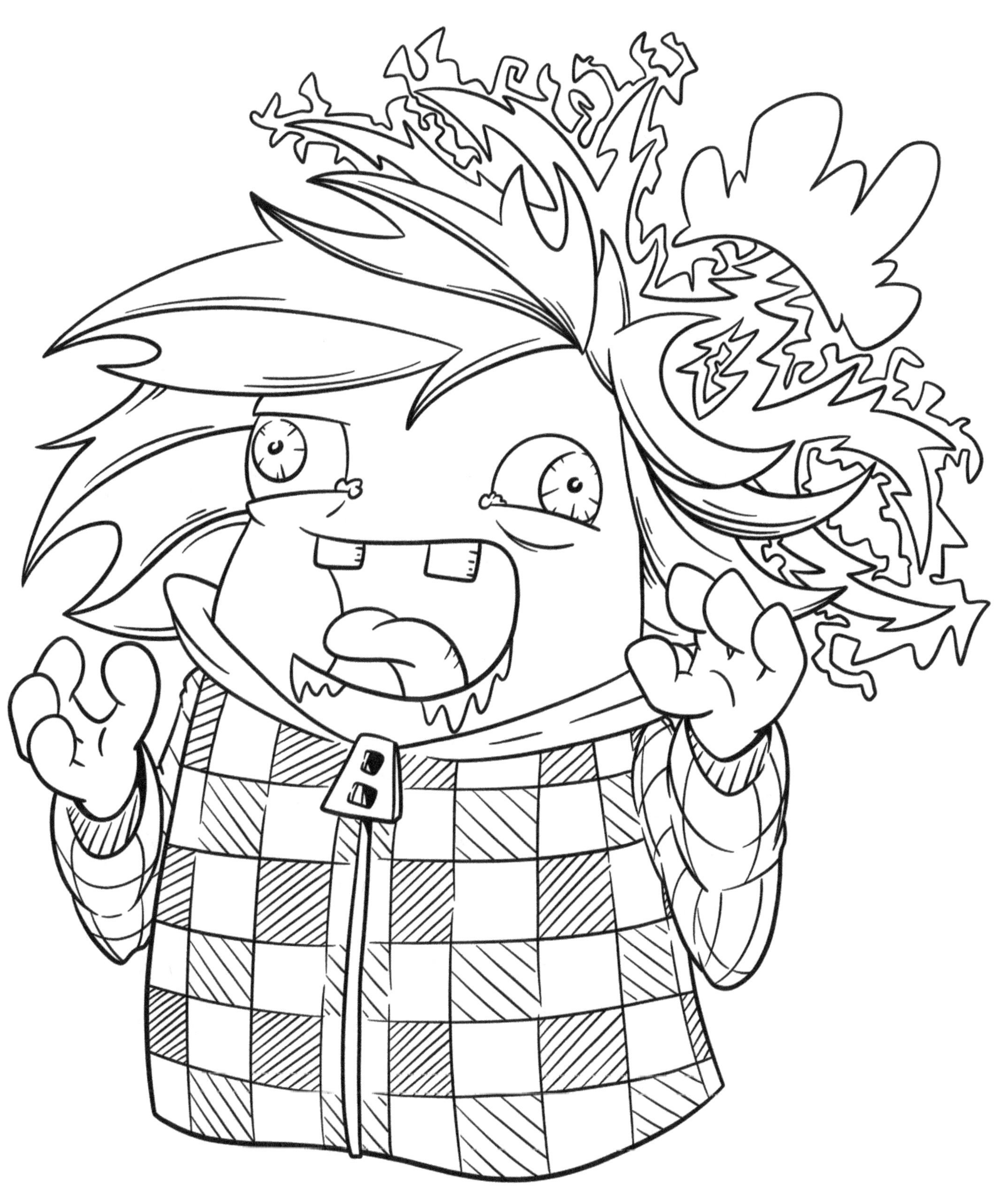

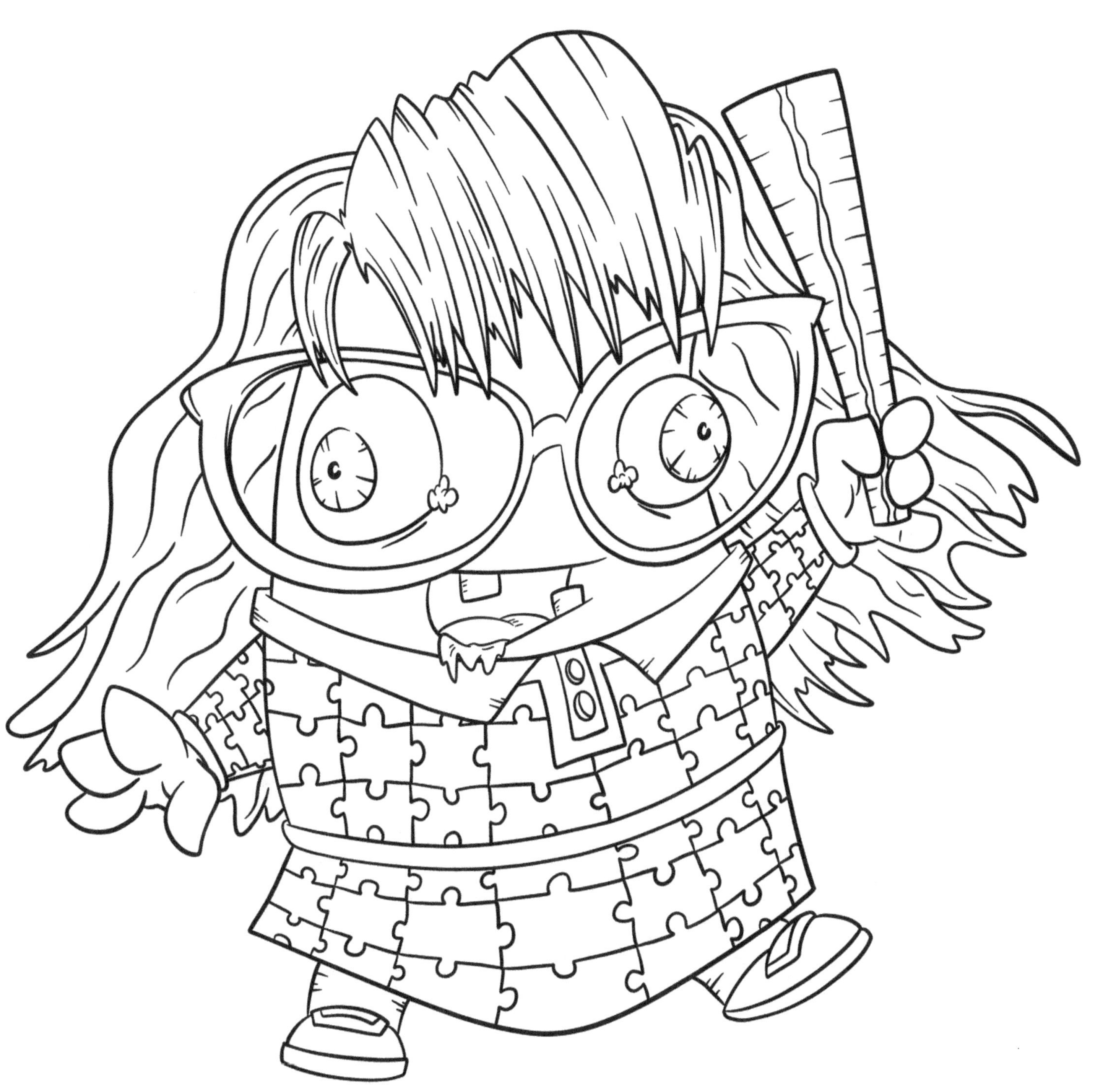

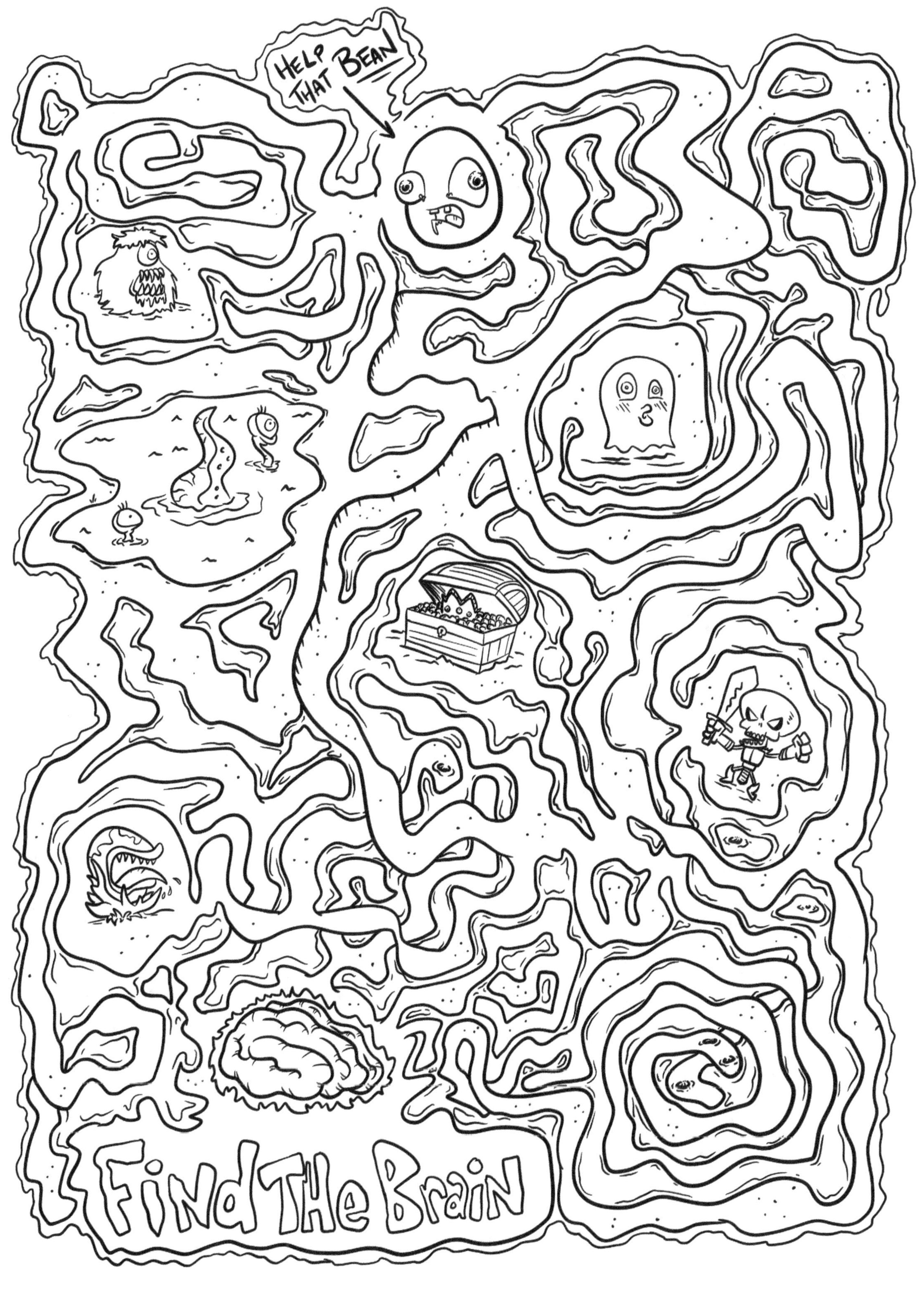

HELP THAT BEAN
FiND THE BRAiN

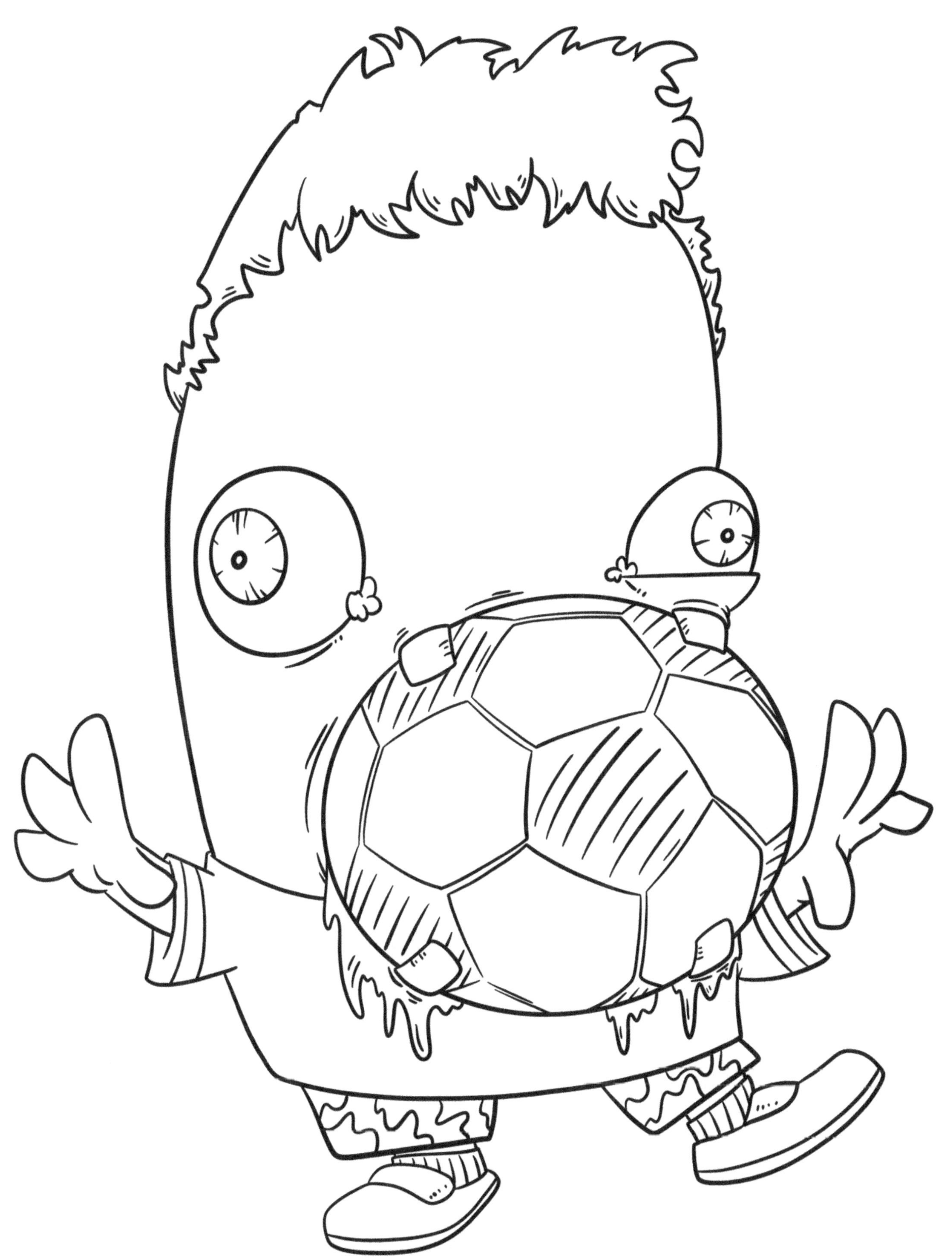

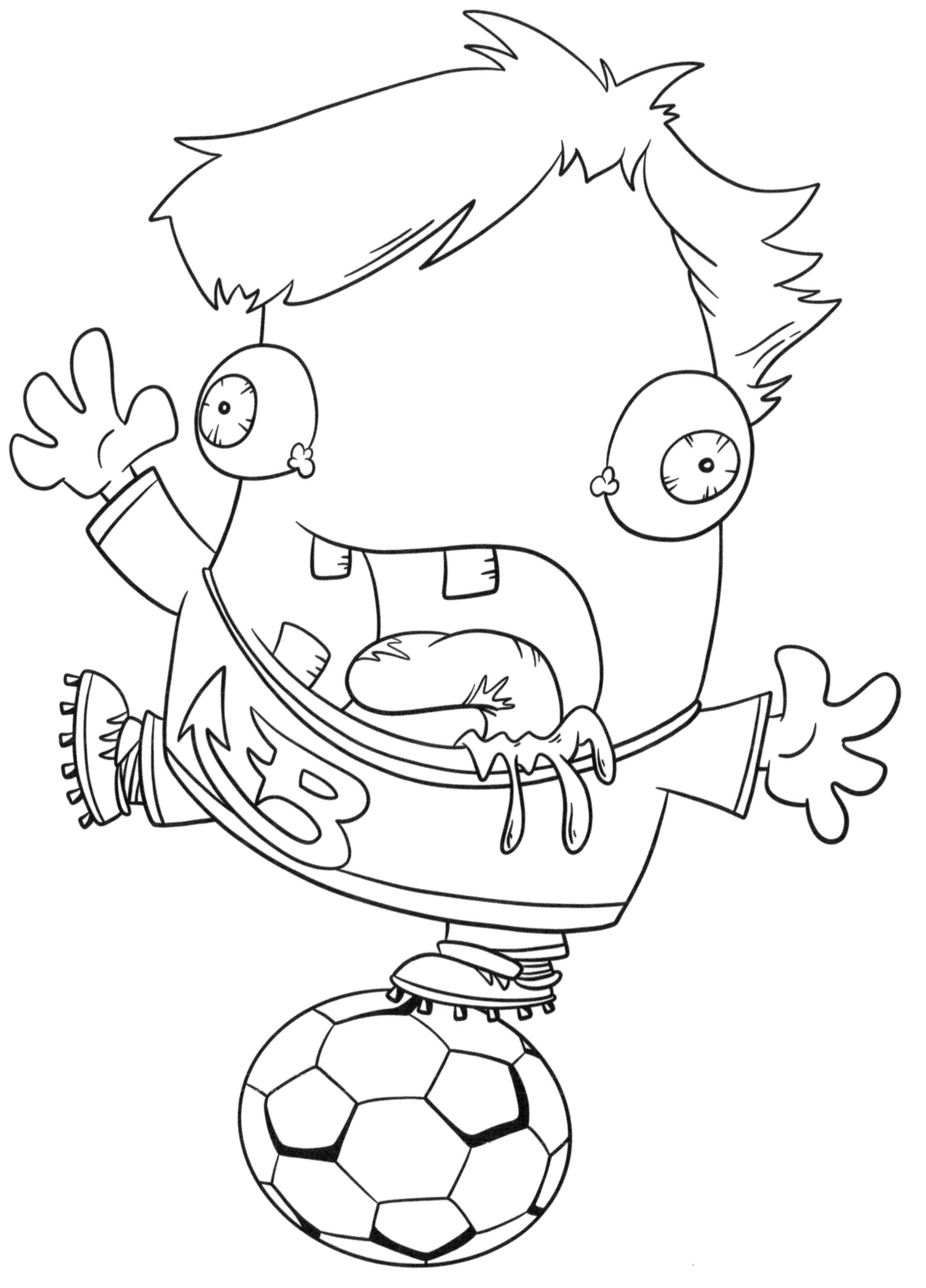
B

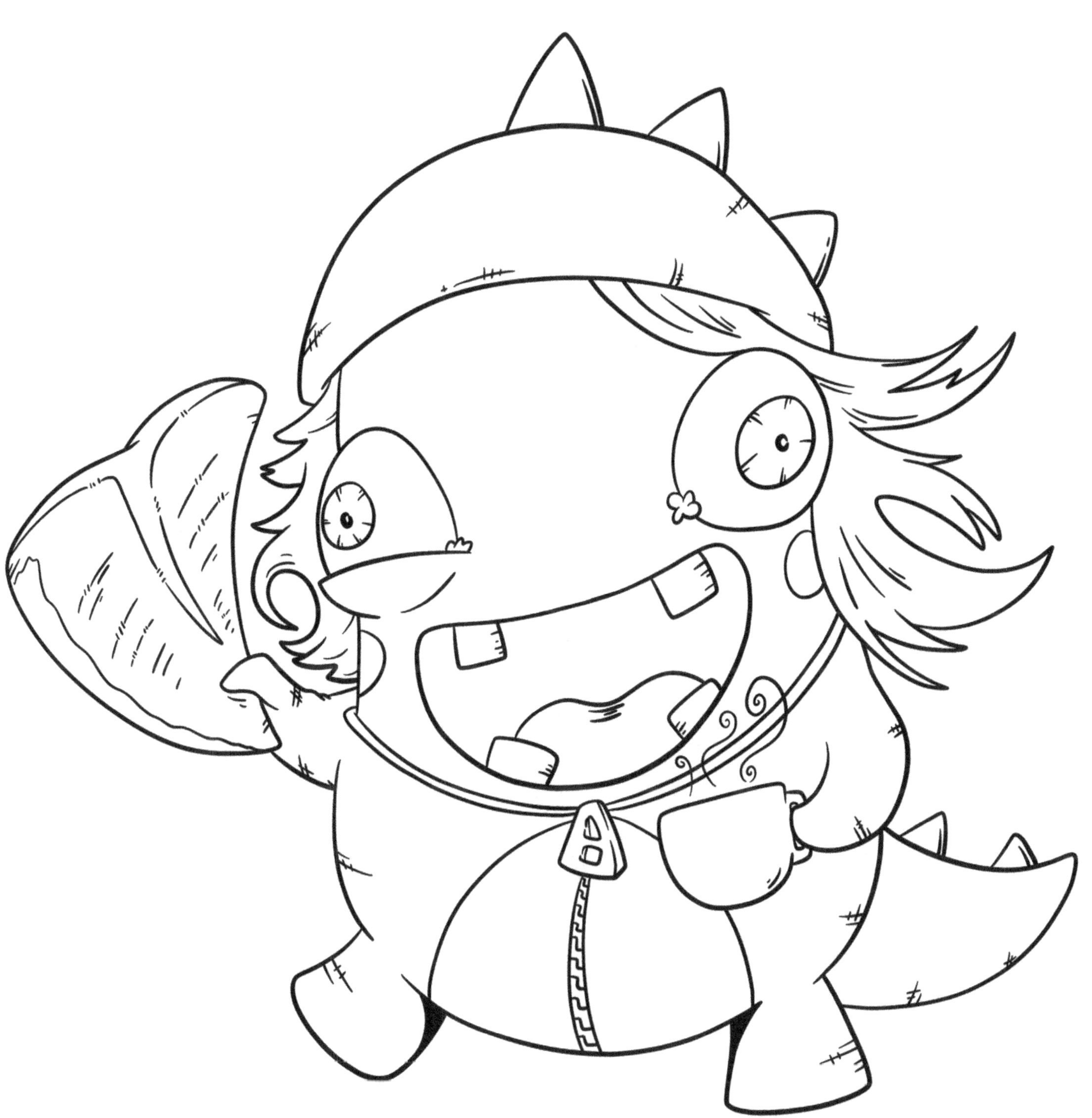

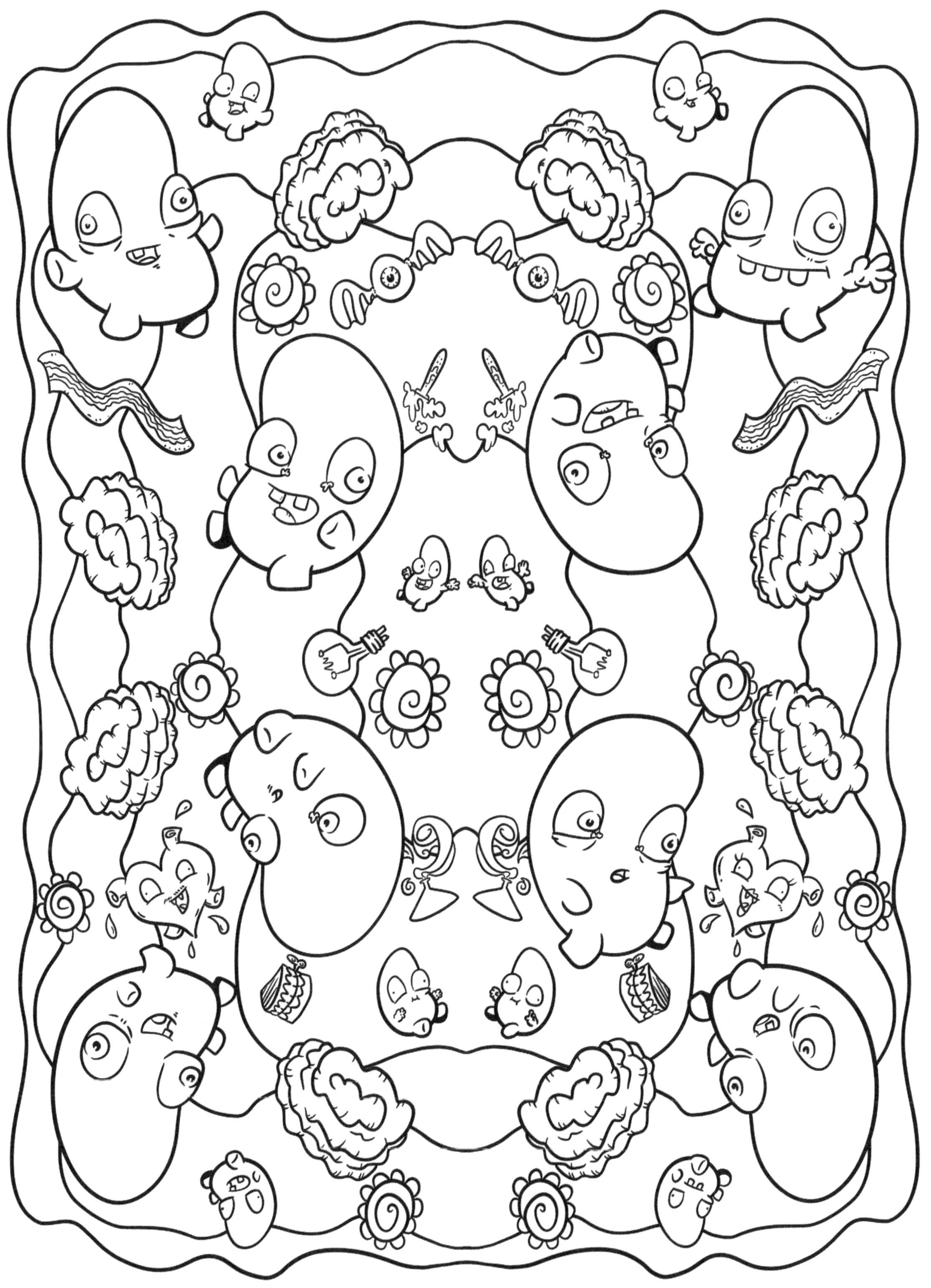

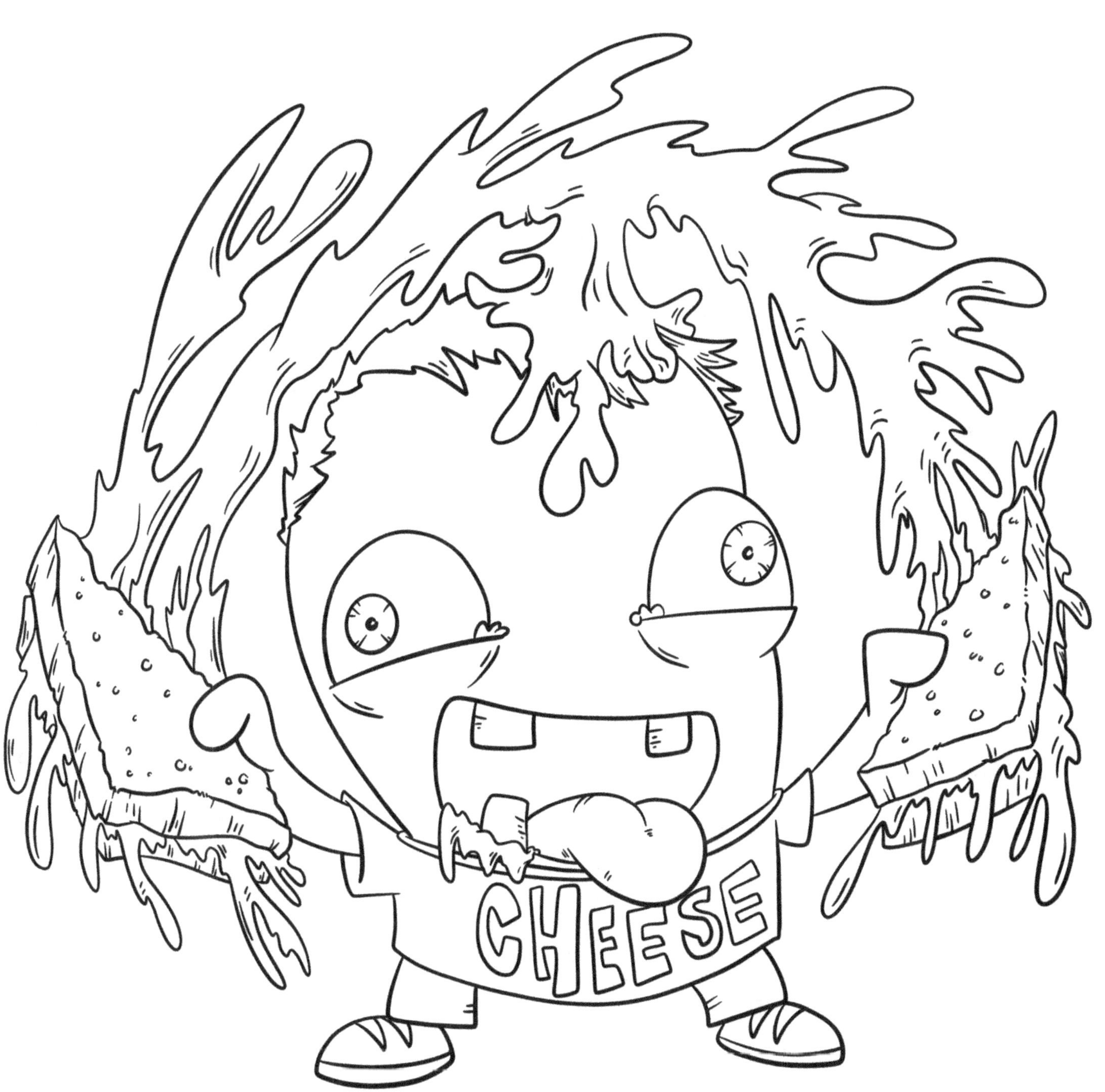

CHEESE

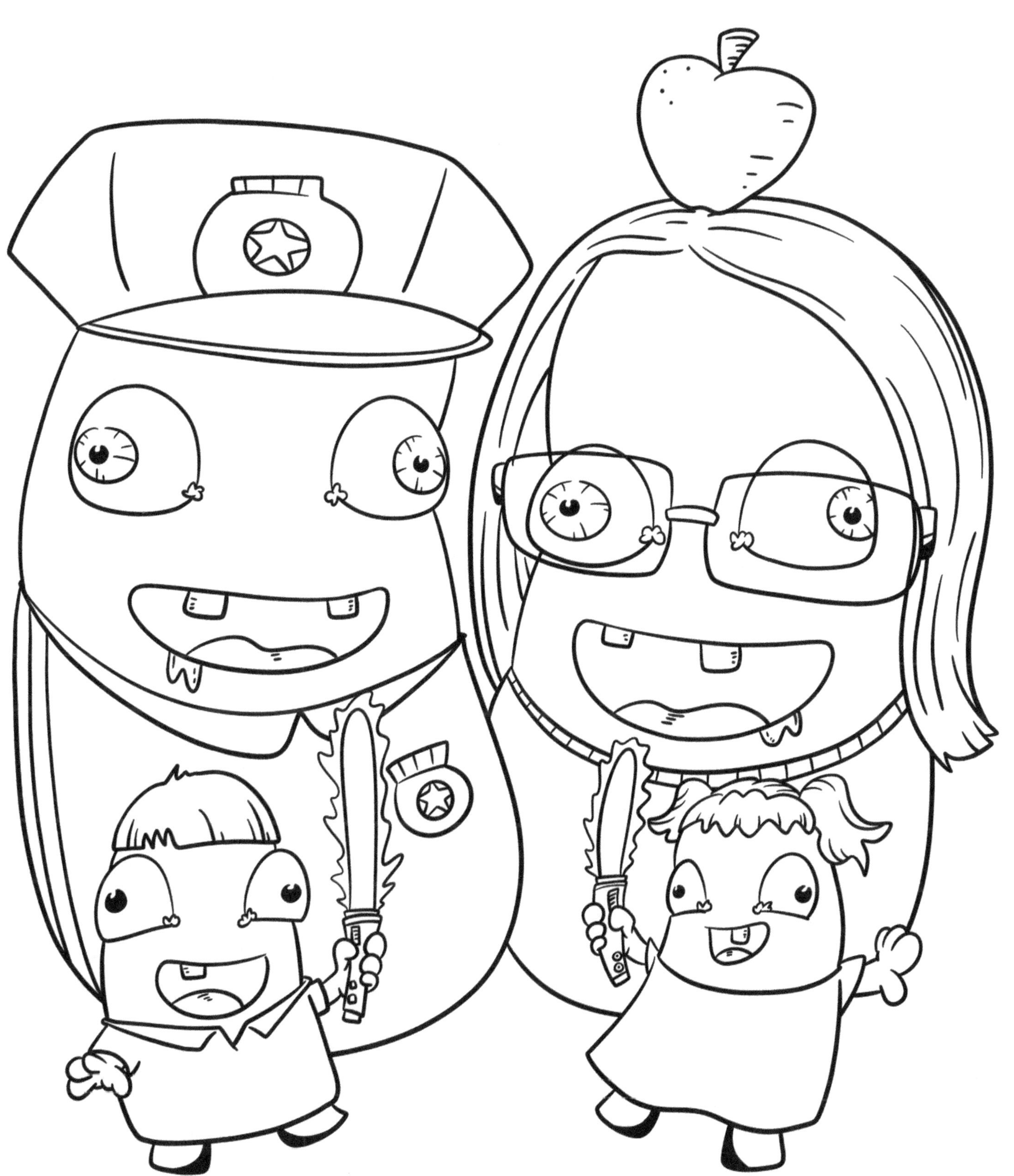

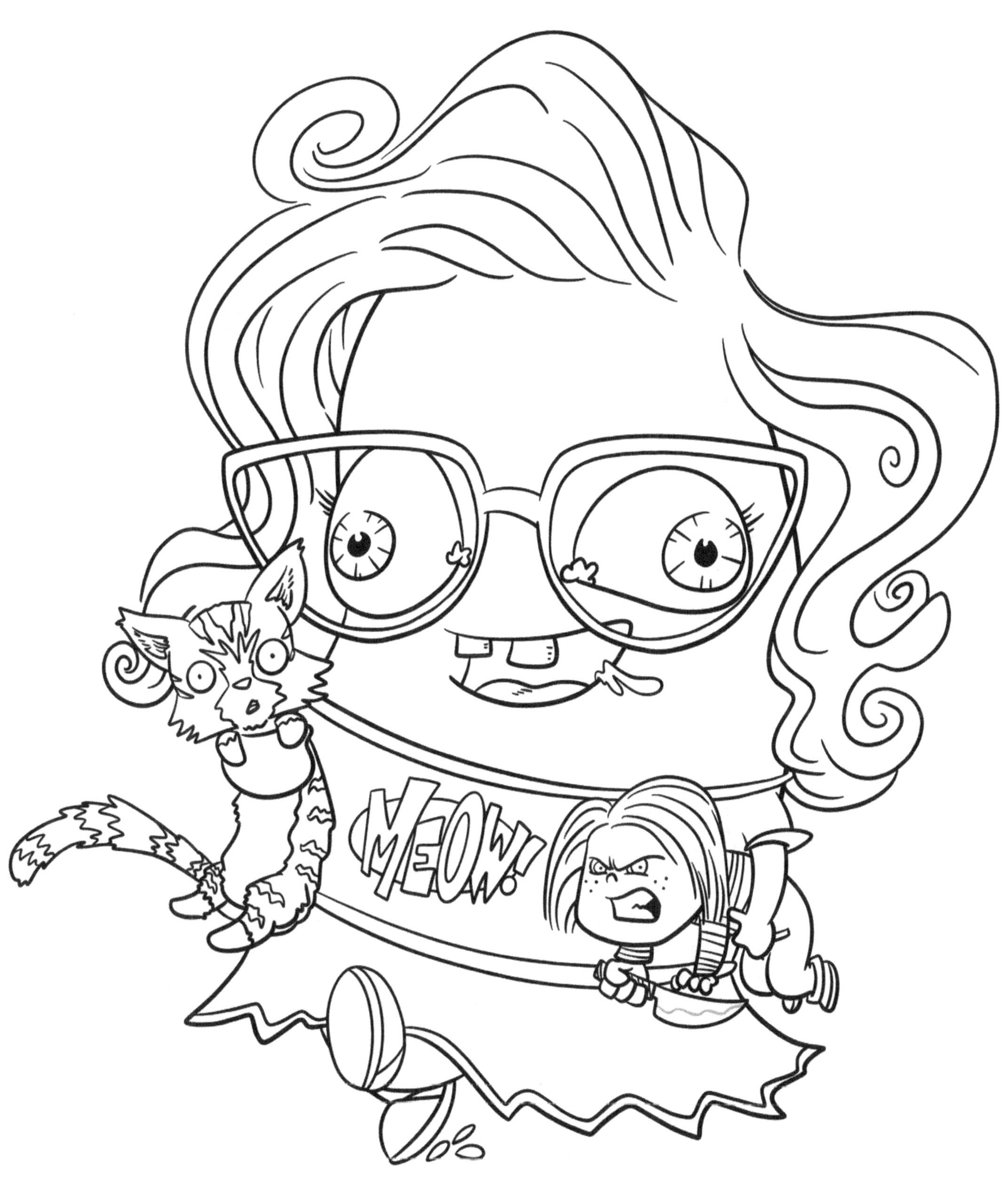

MEOW!

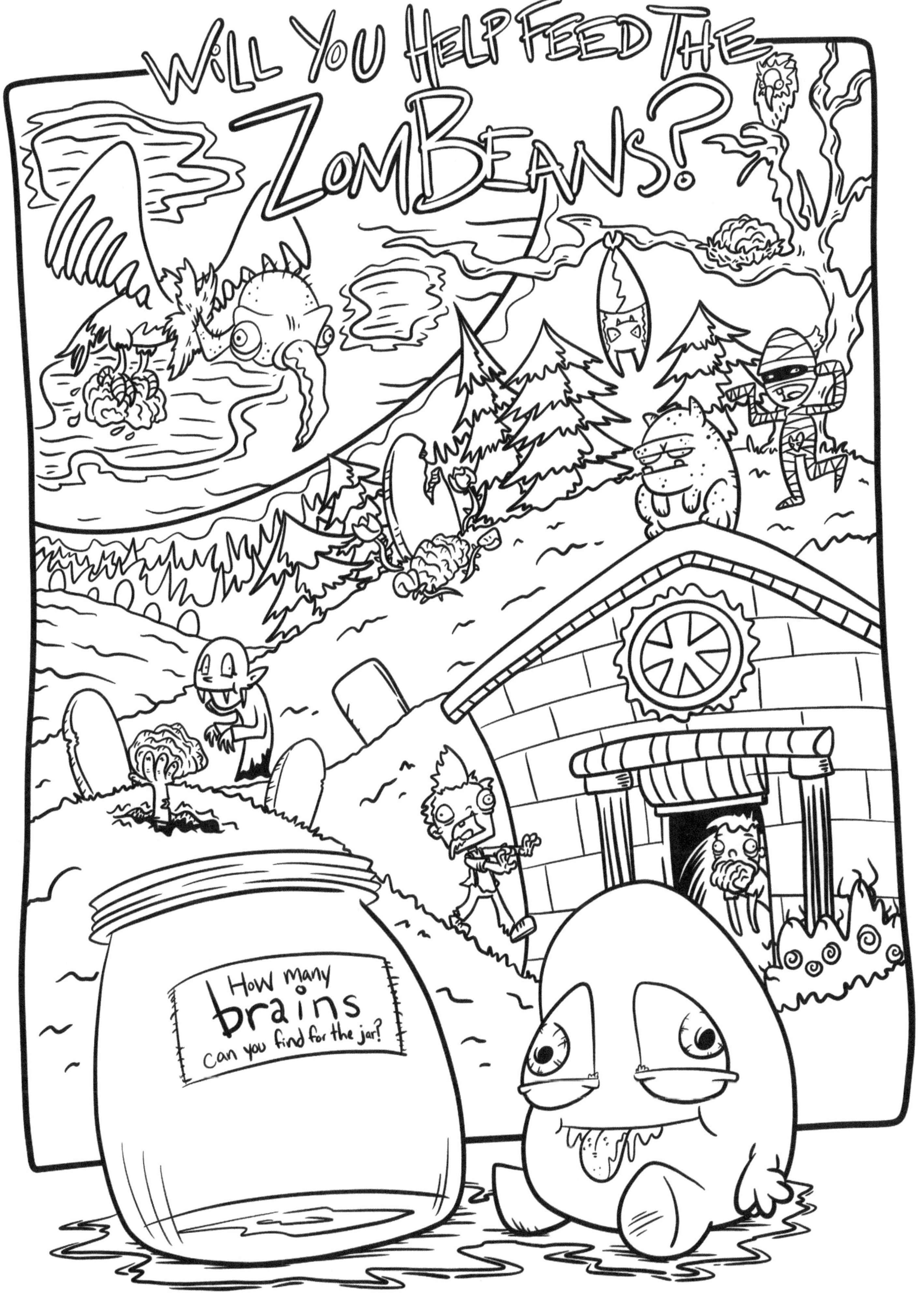

WILL YOU HELP FEED THE ZomBeans?
How many brains can you find for the jar?

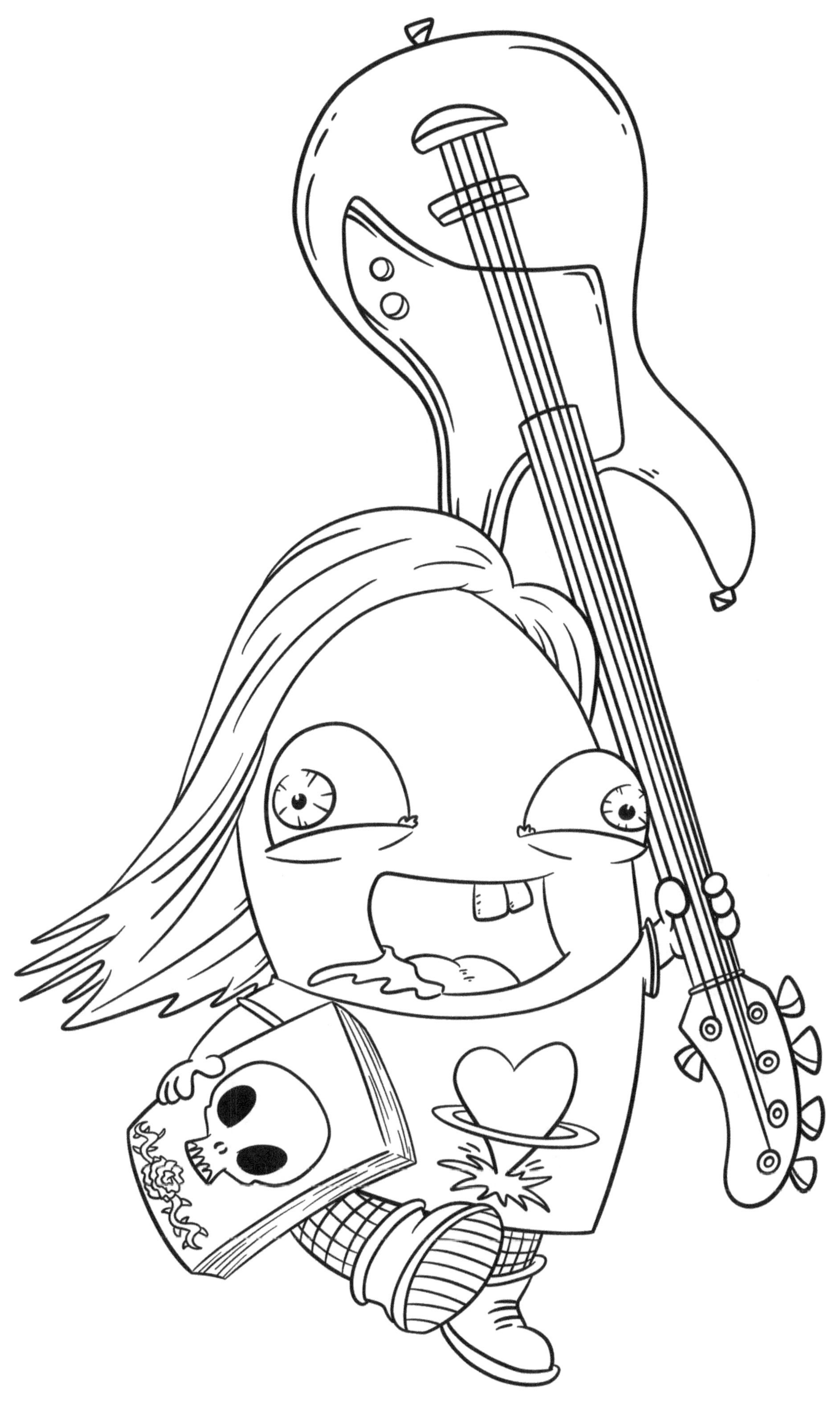

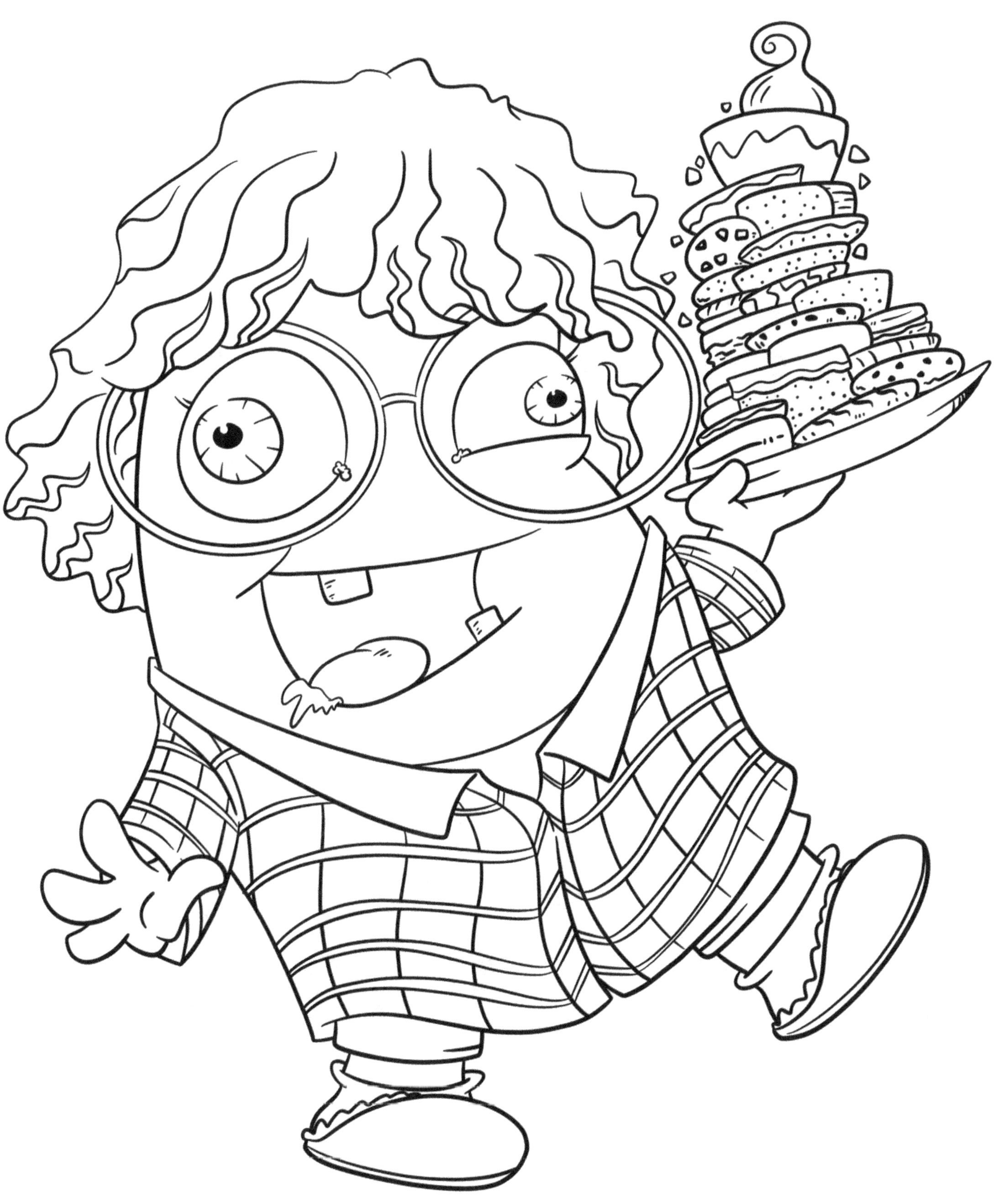

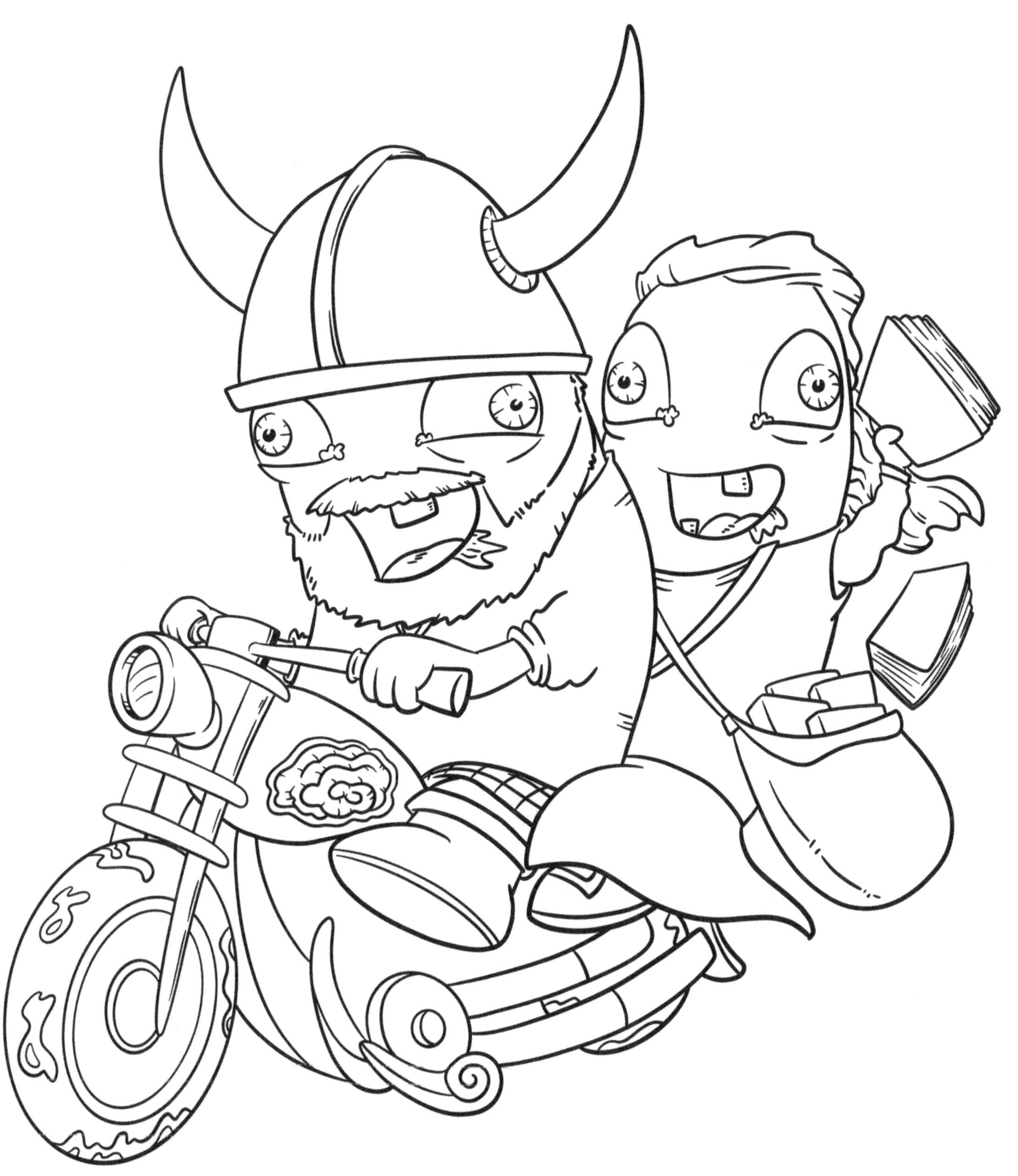

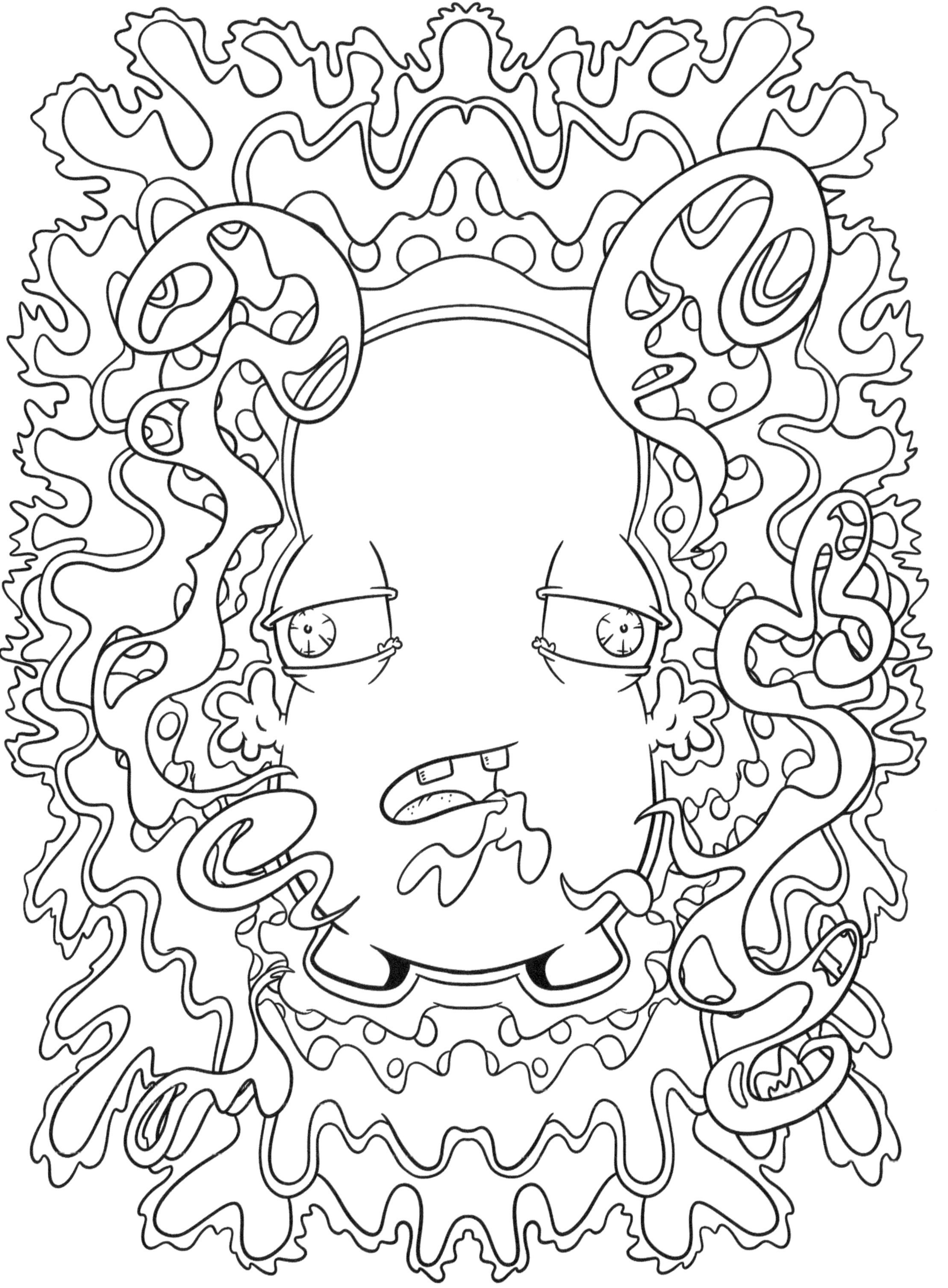

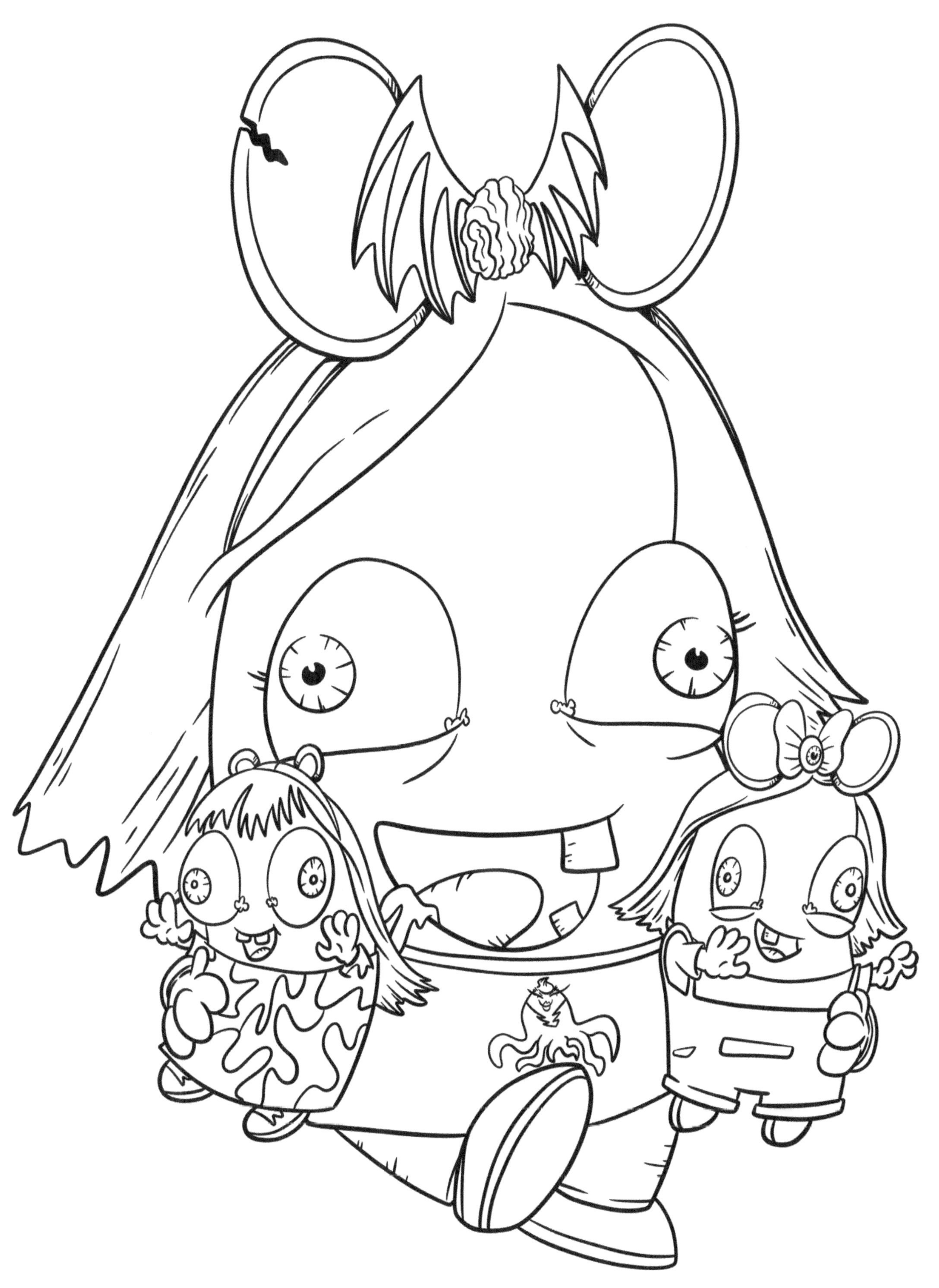

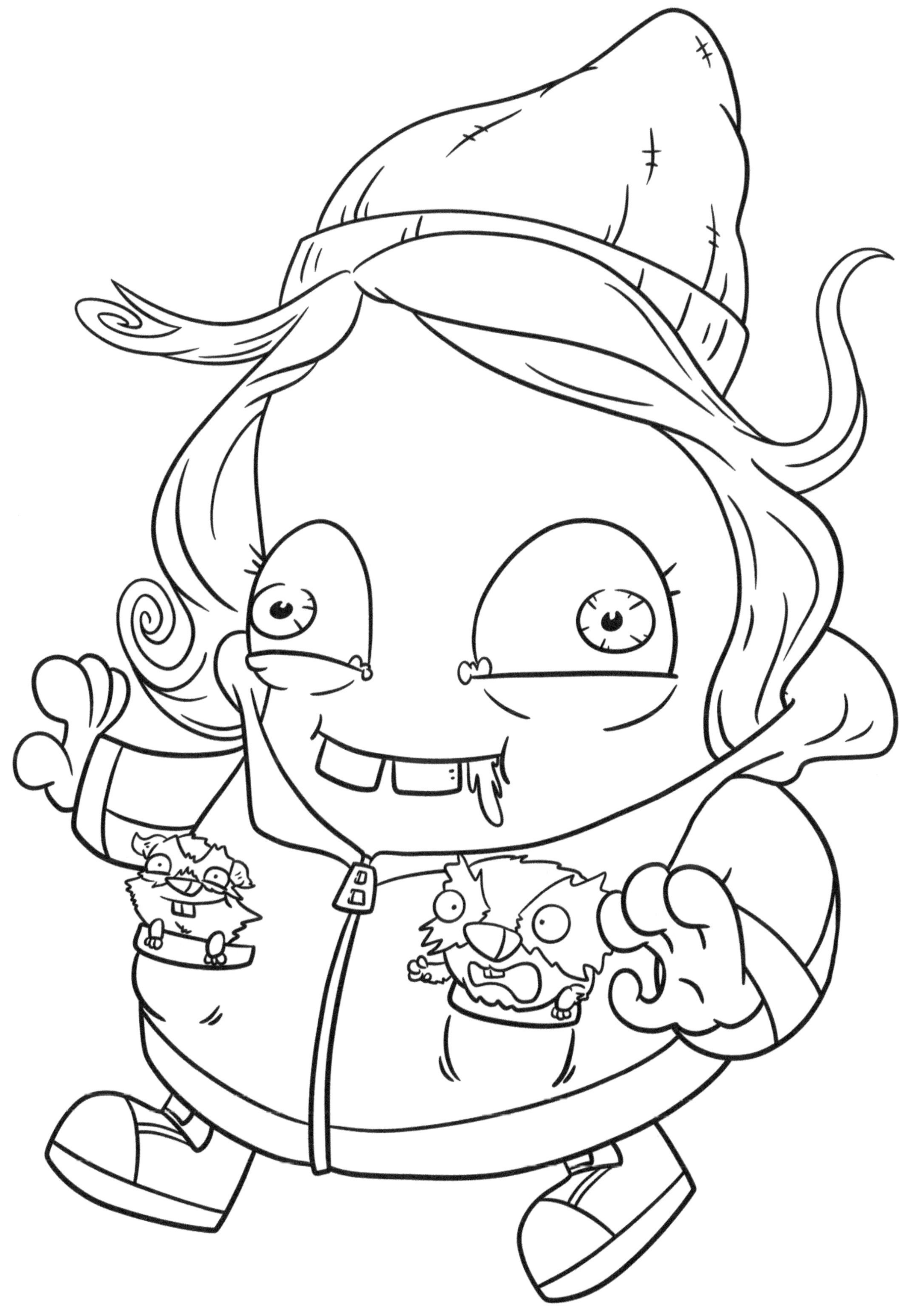

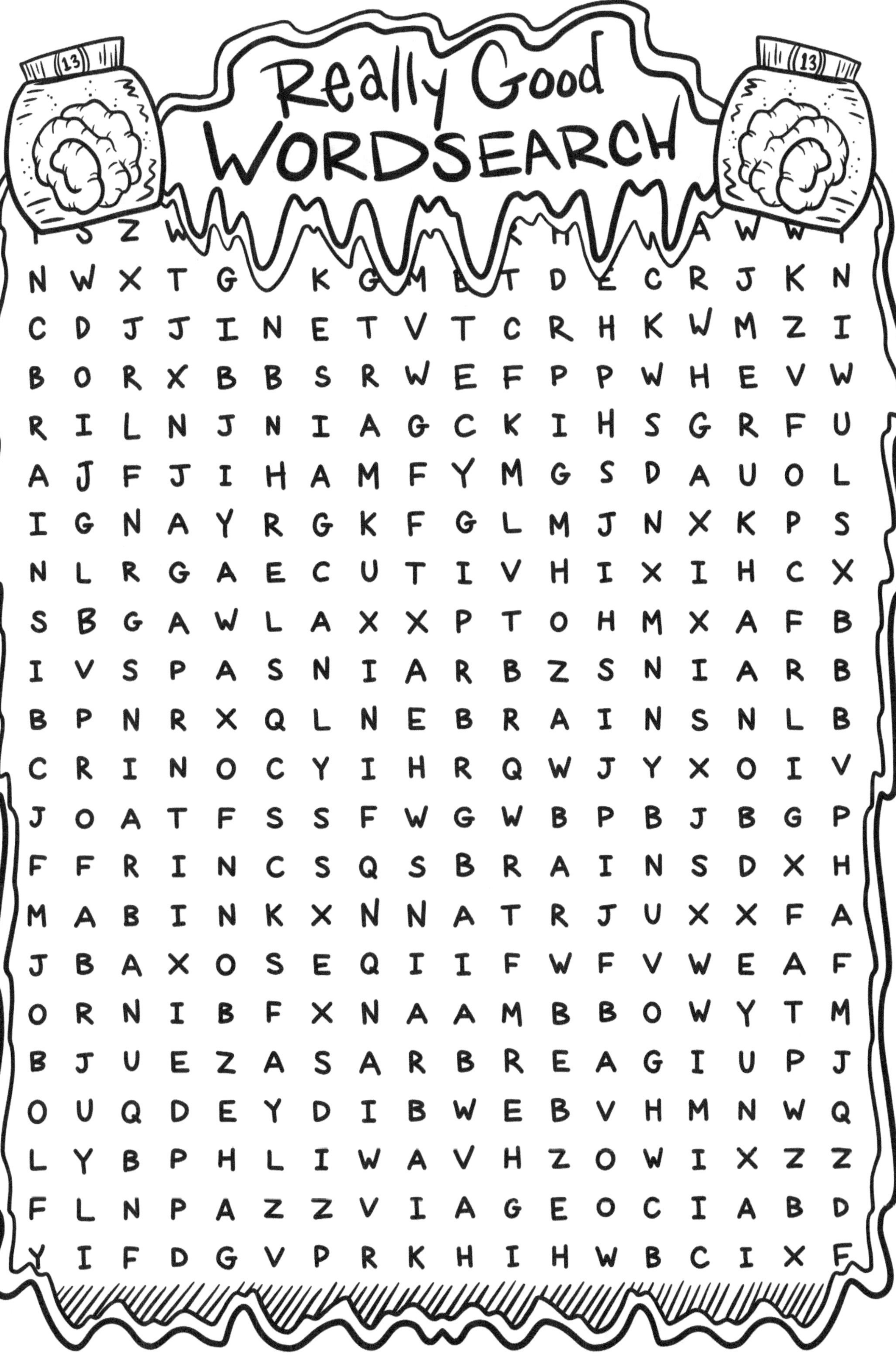

Really Good
WORDSEARCH

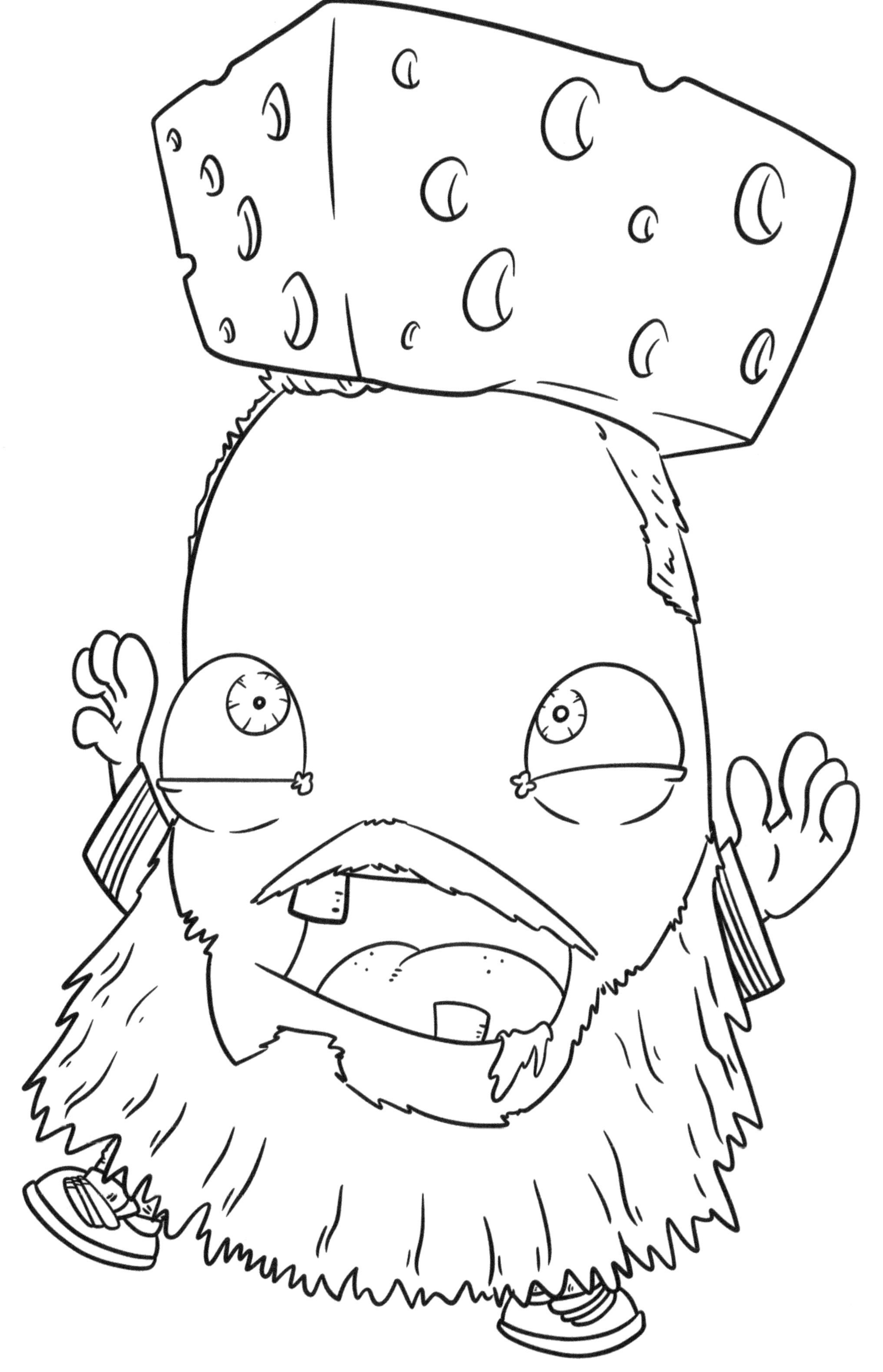

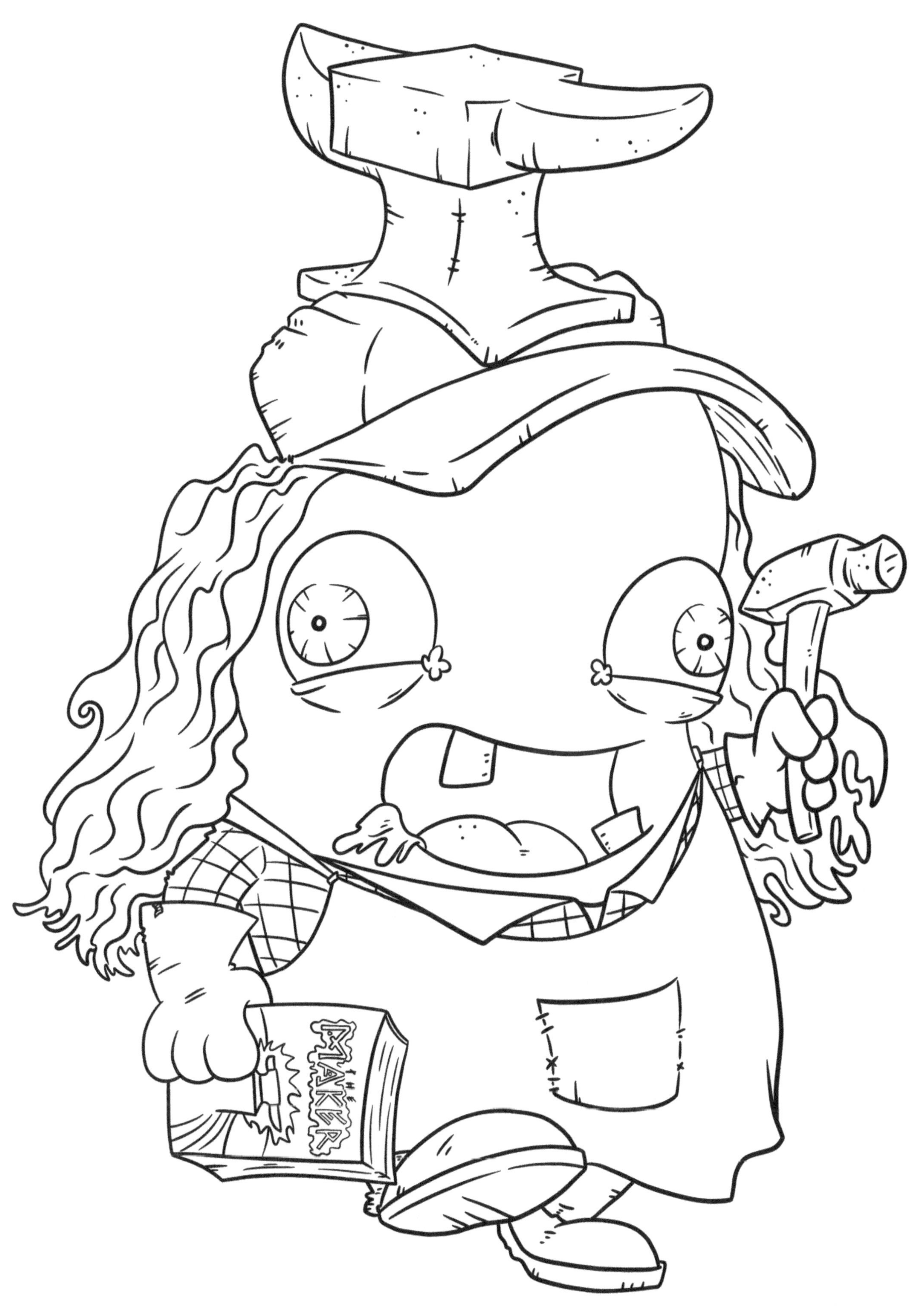

THE MAKER

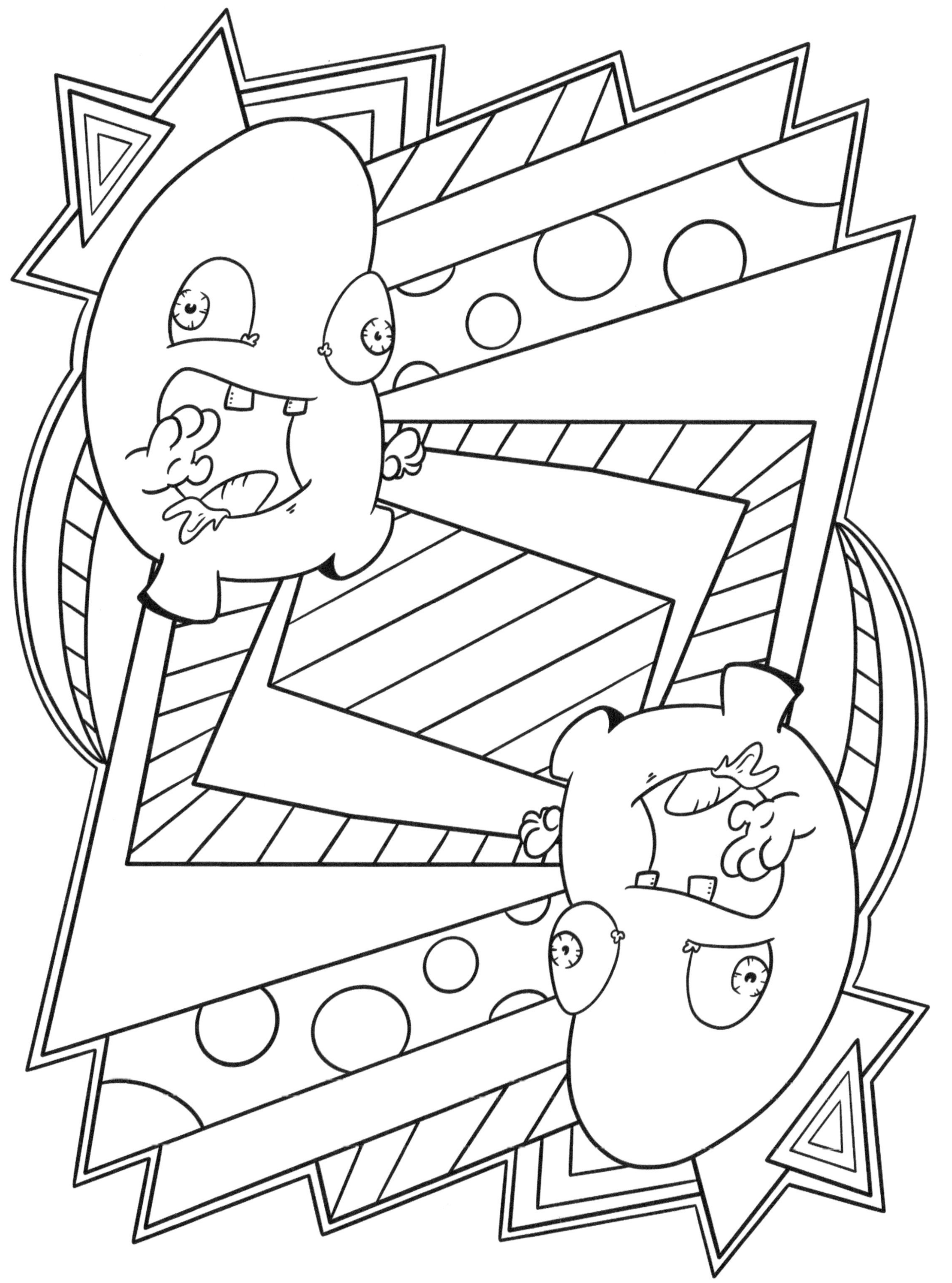

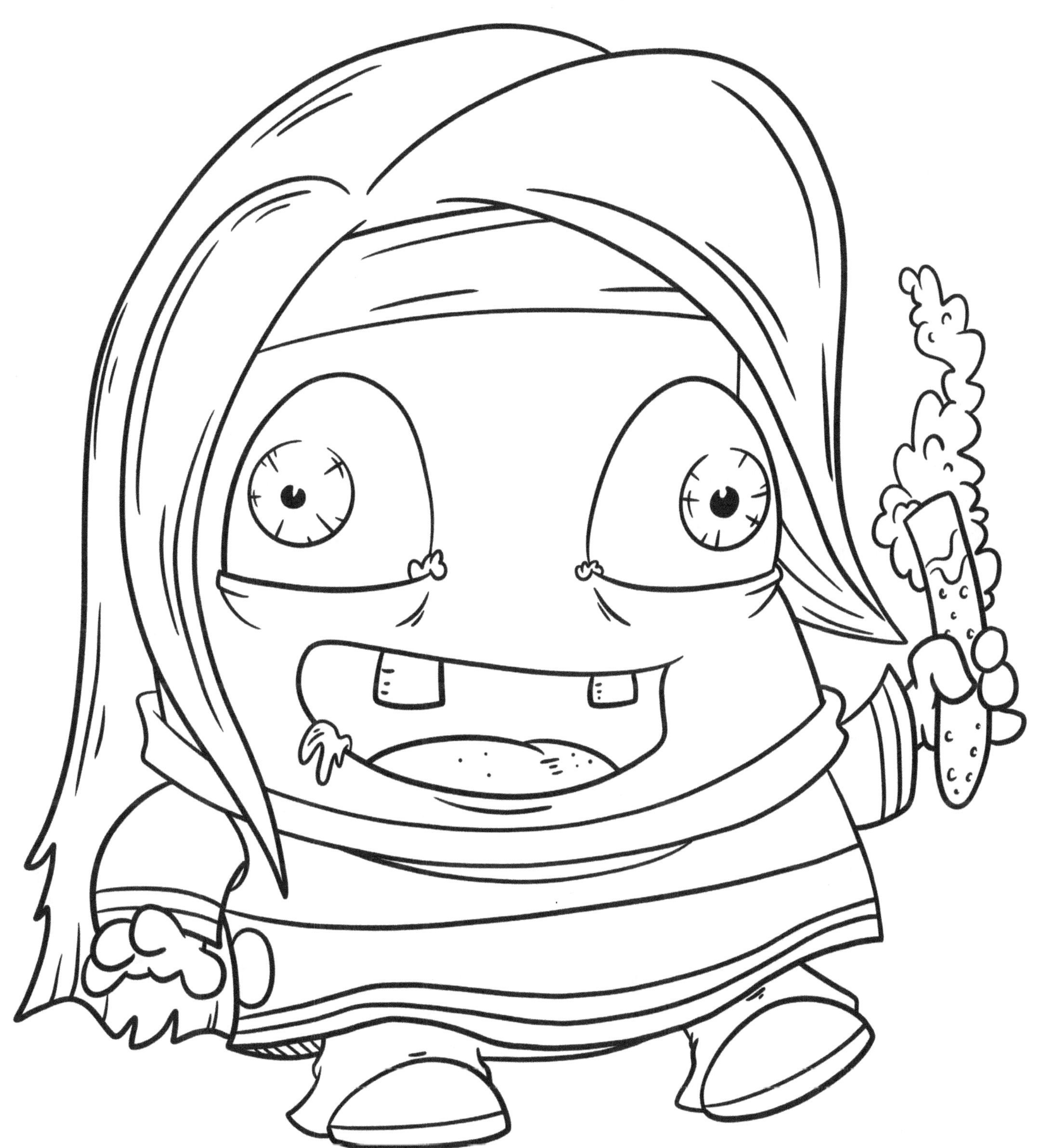

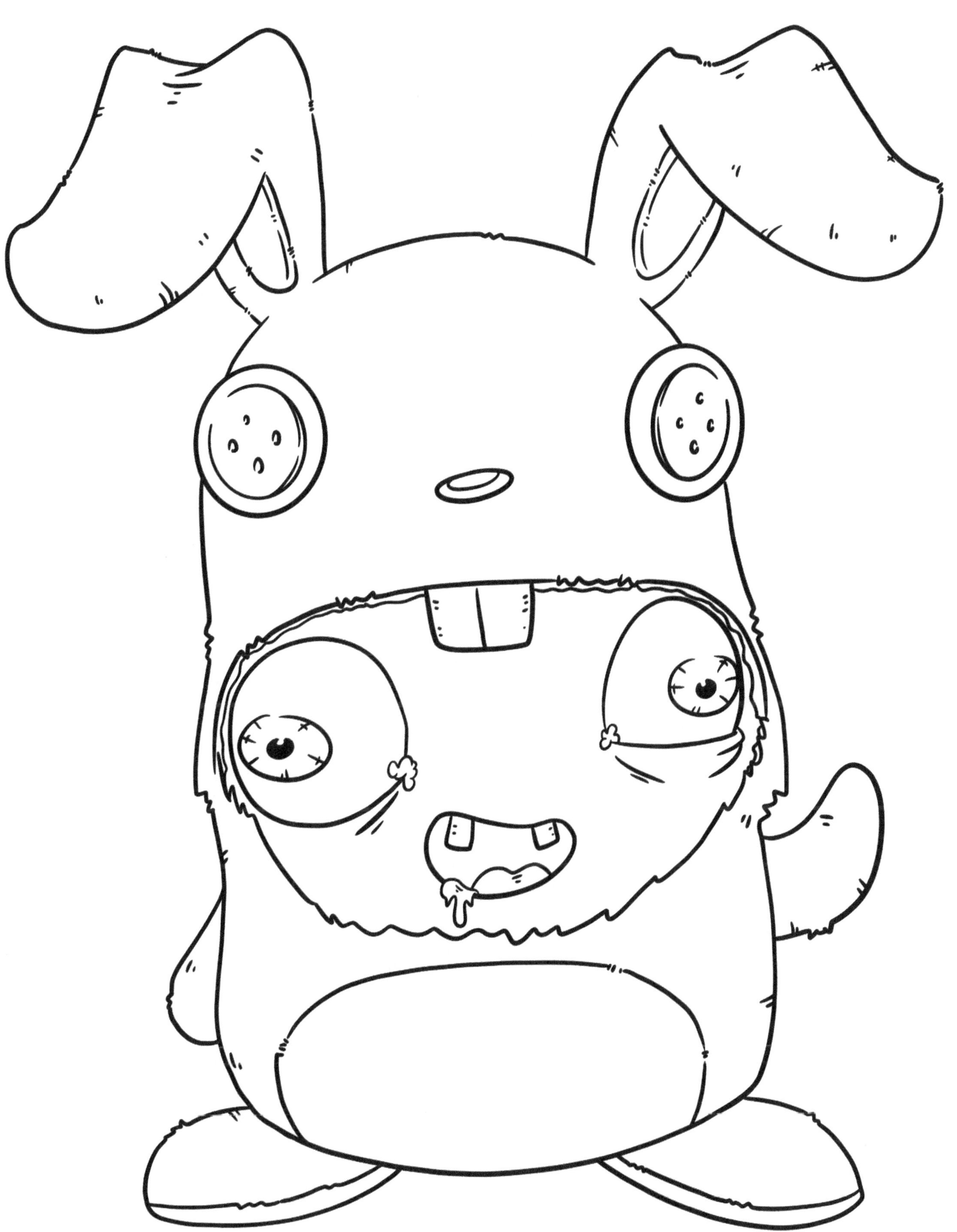

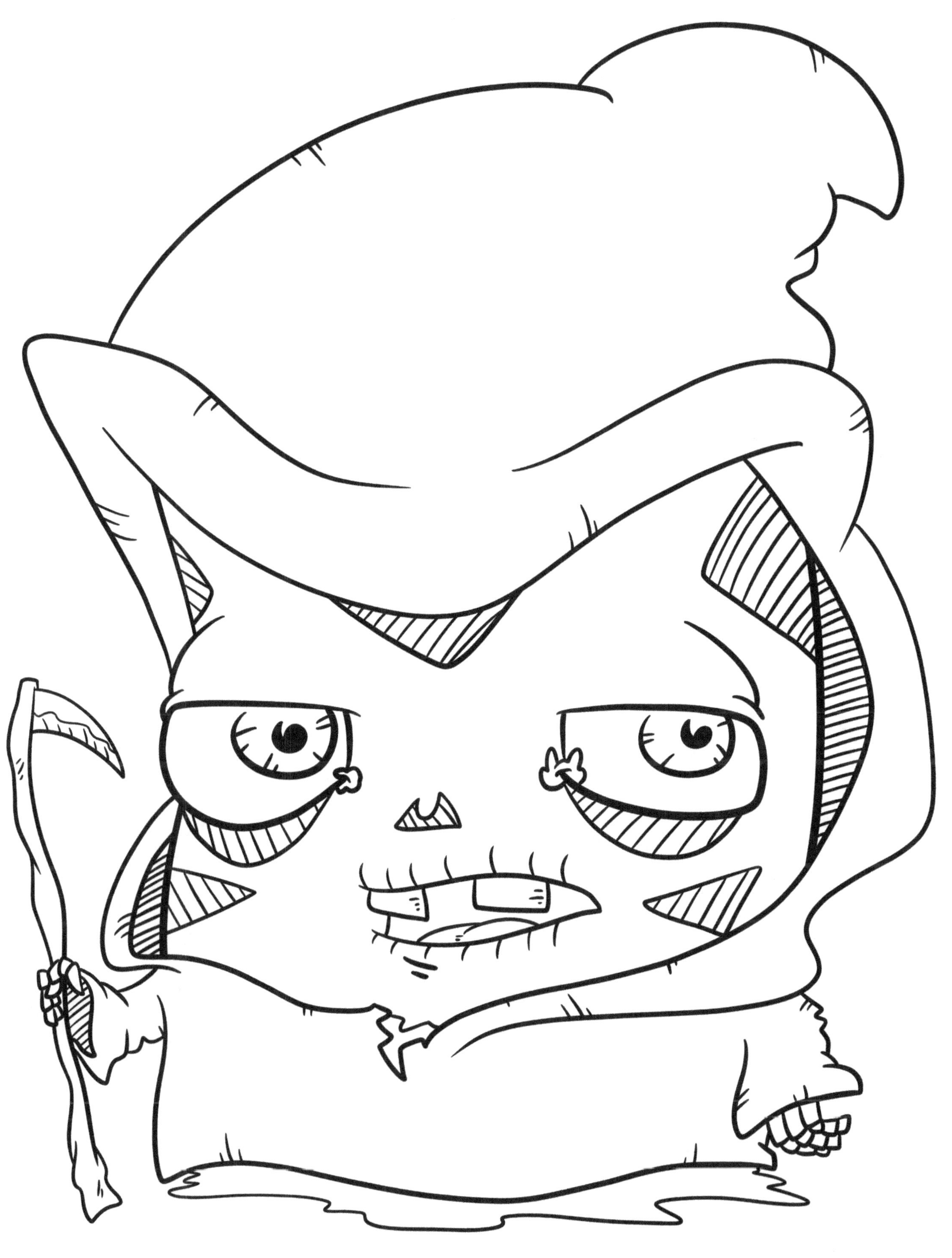

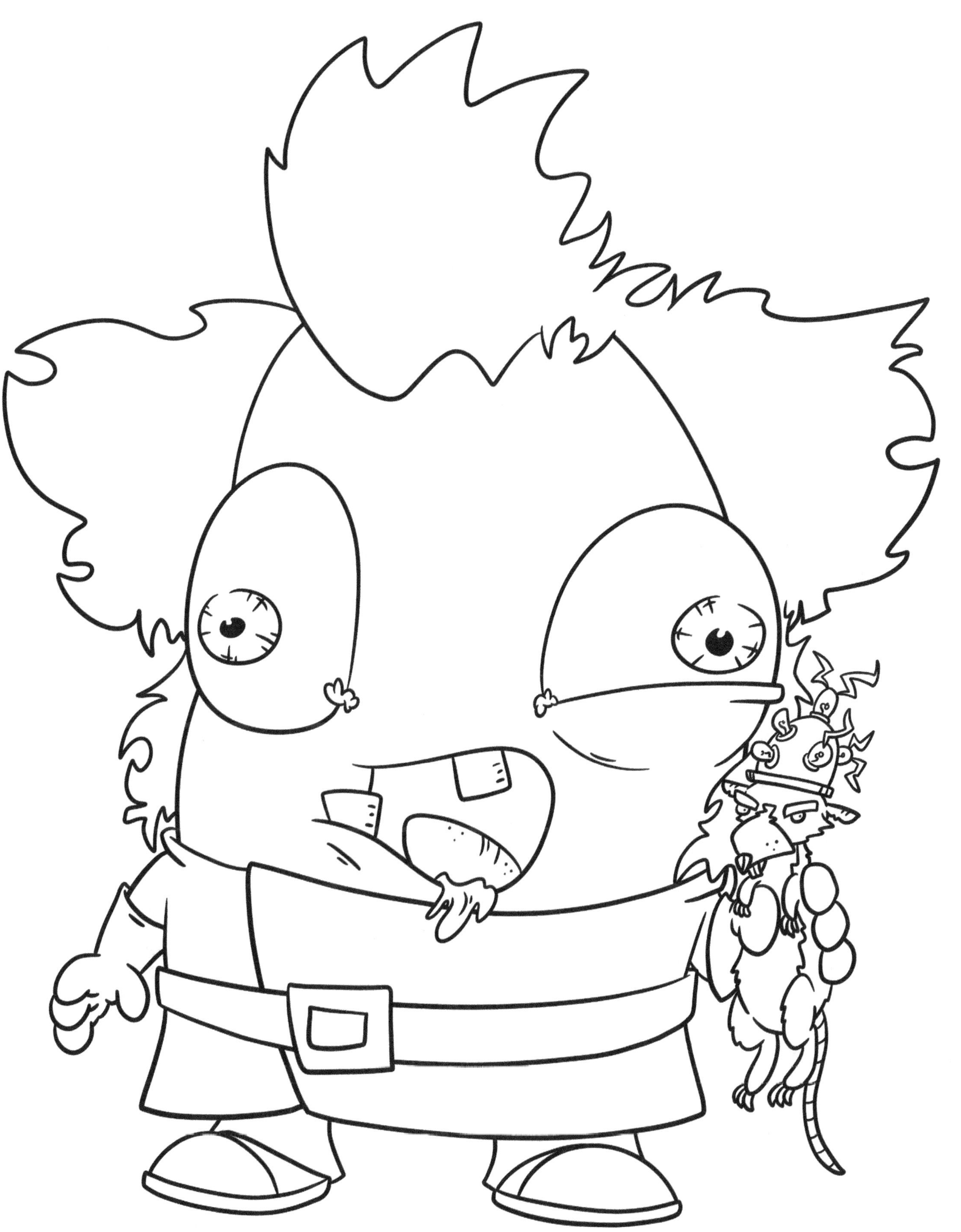

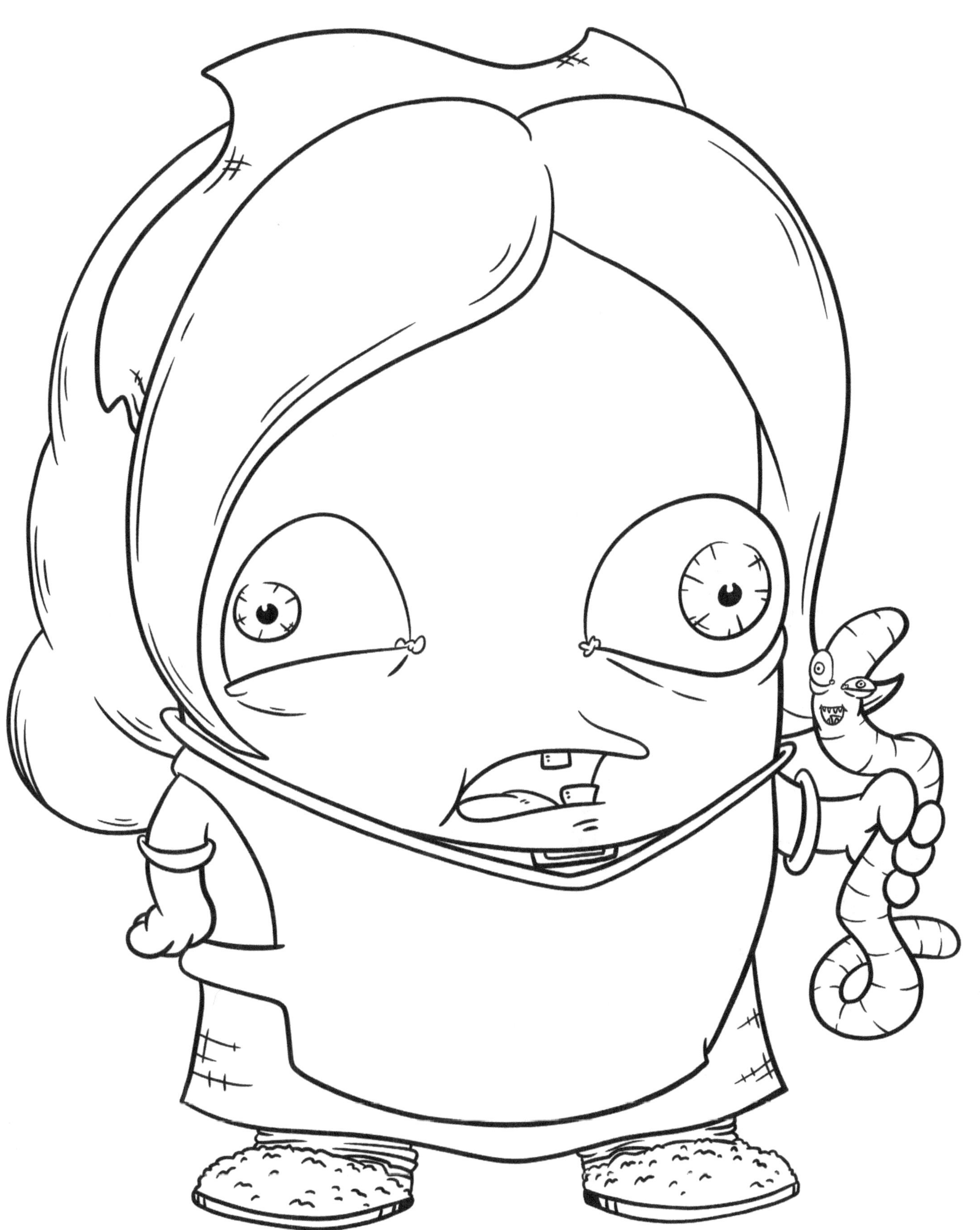

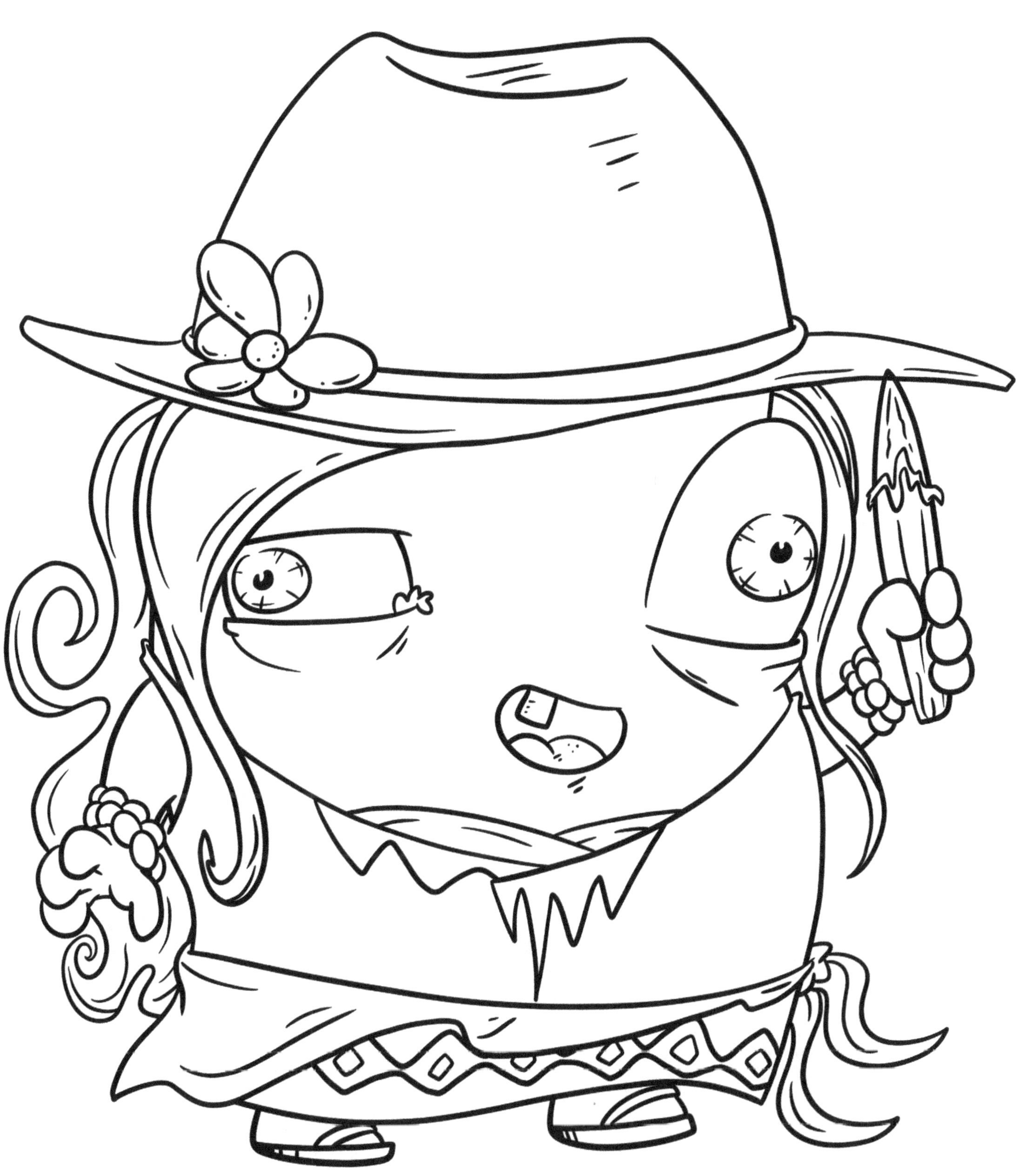

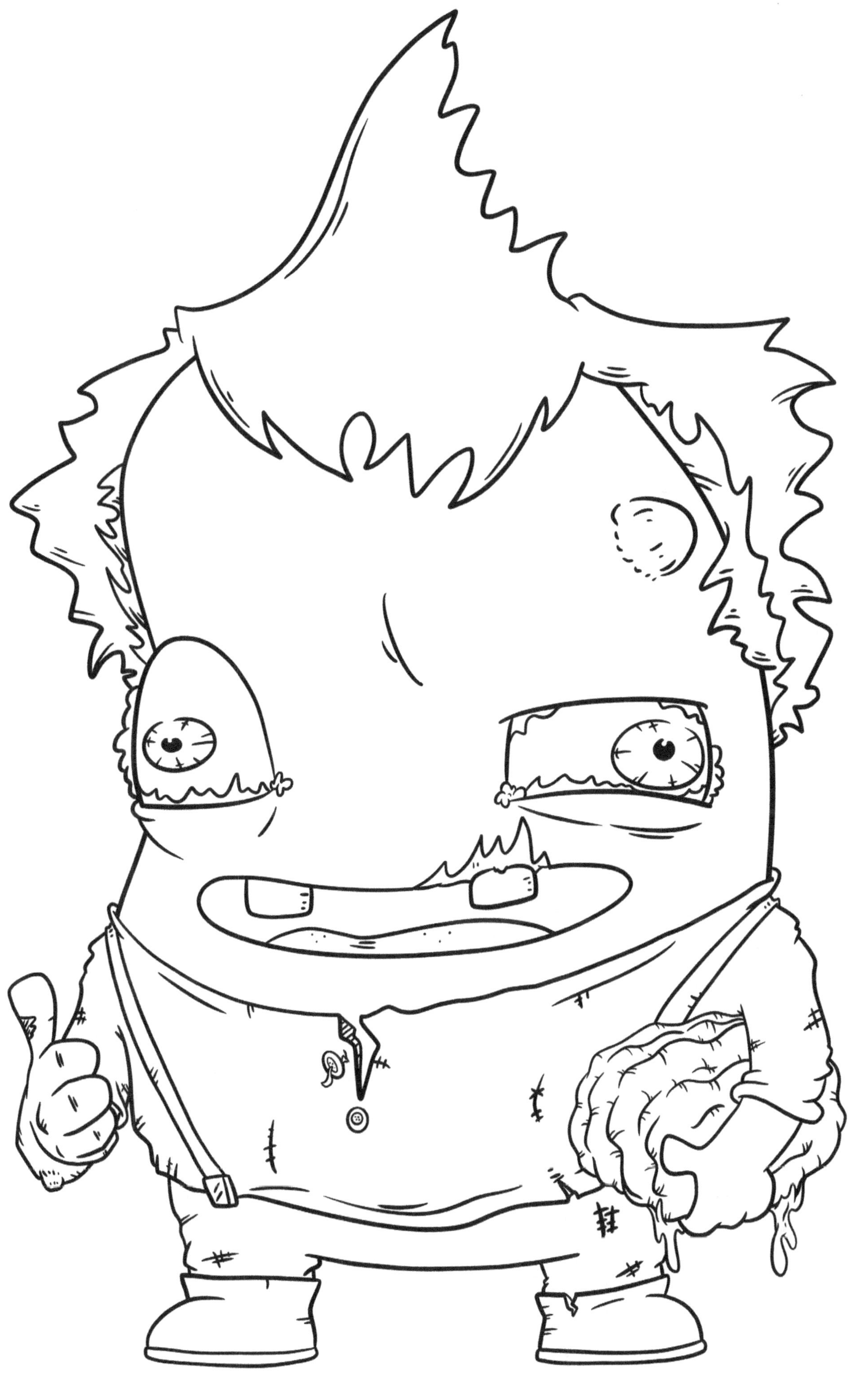

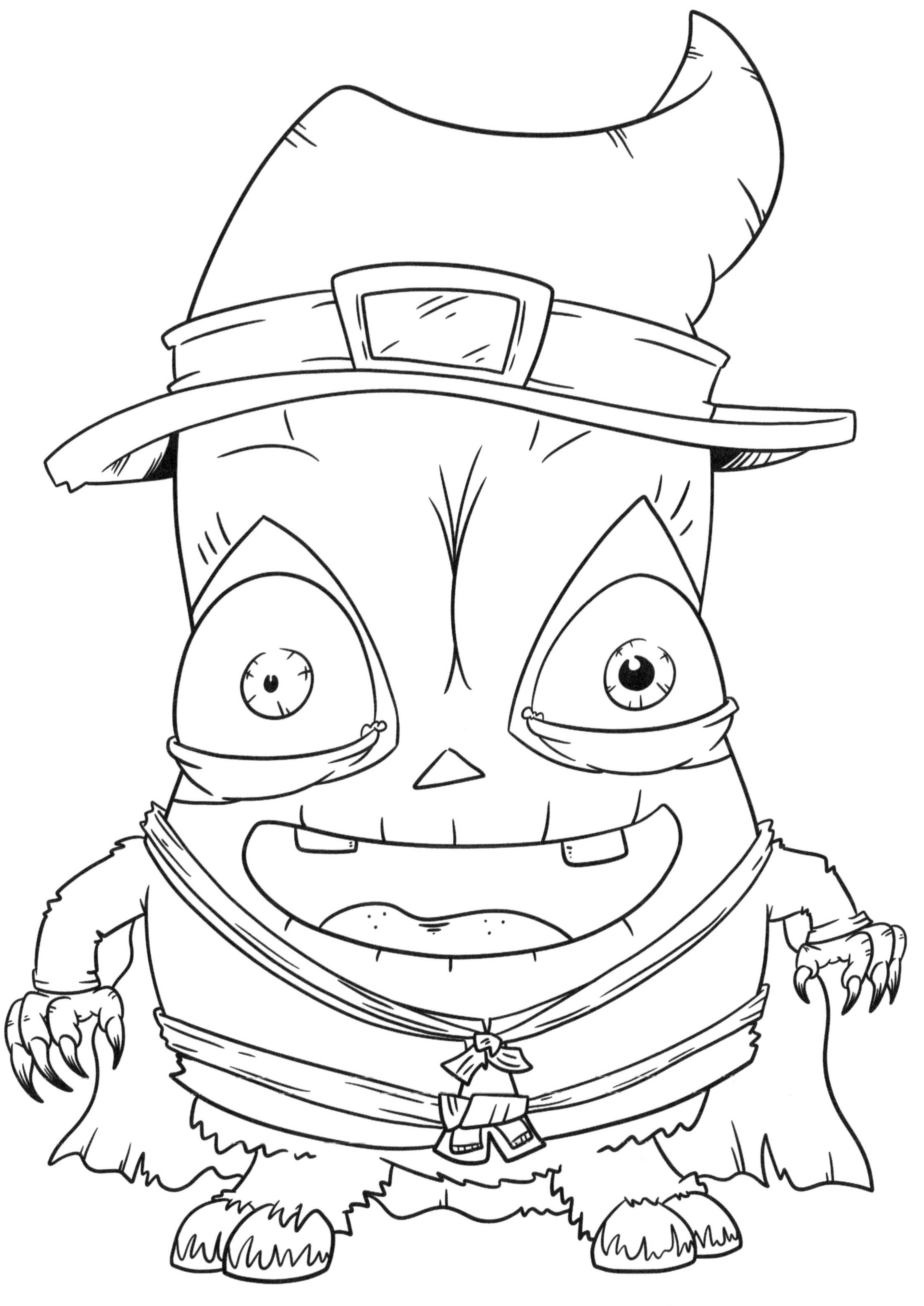

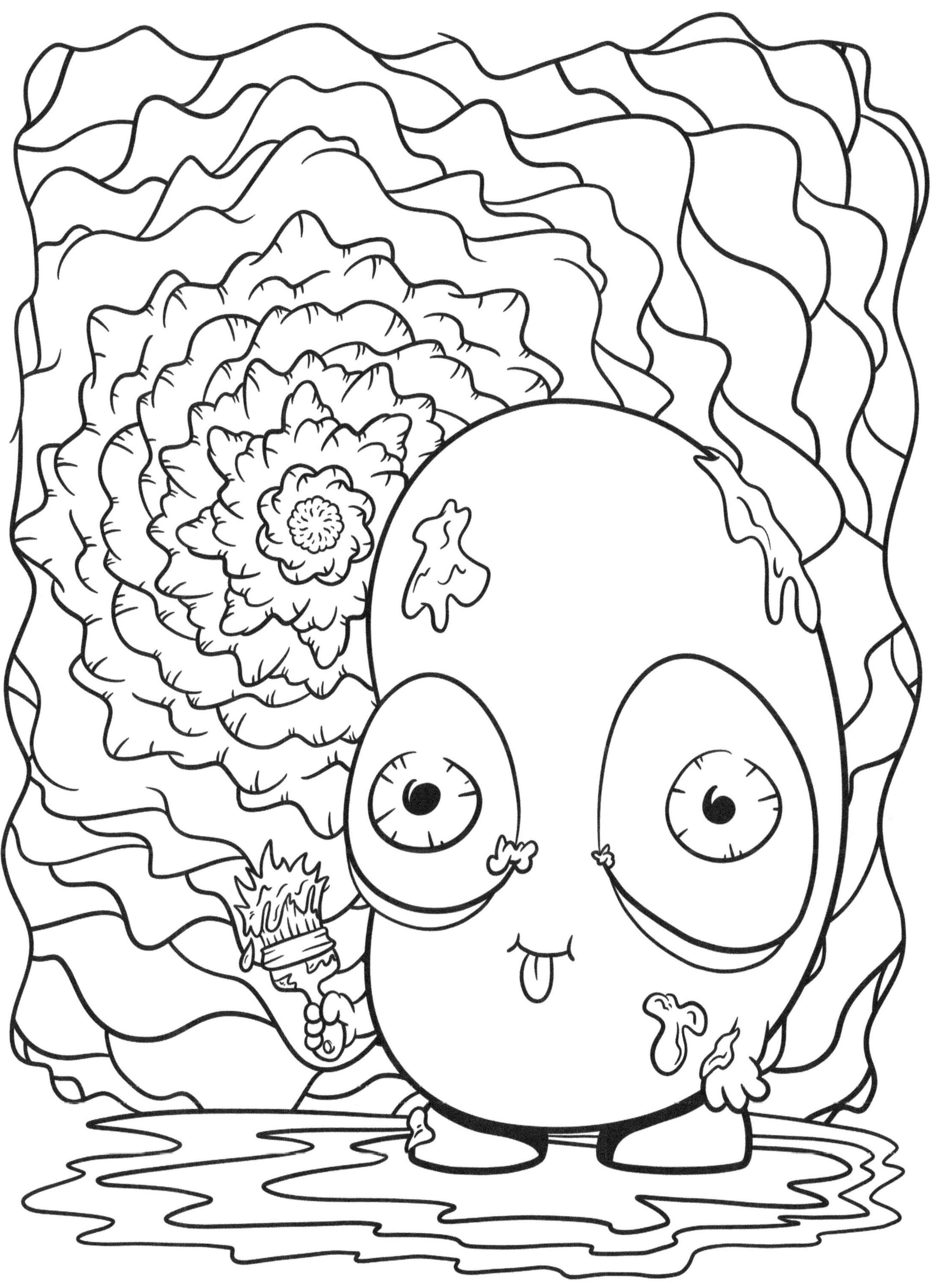

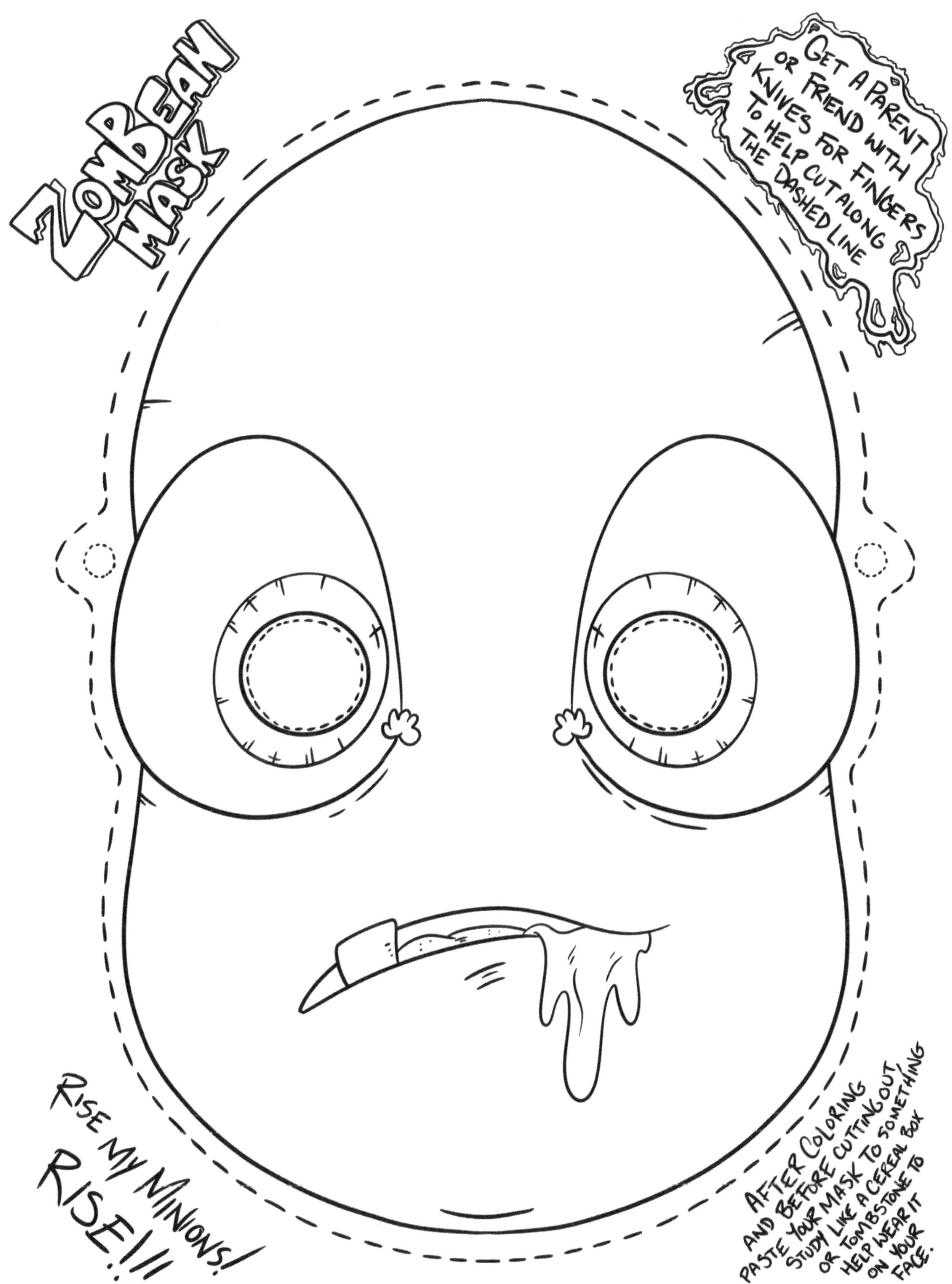

ZomBean Mask
Get a parent or friend with knives for fingers to help cut along the dashed line
Rise my minions! Rise!!!
After coloring and before cutting out paste your mask to something study like a cereal box or tombstone to help wear it on your face.

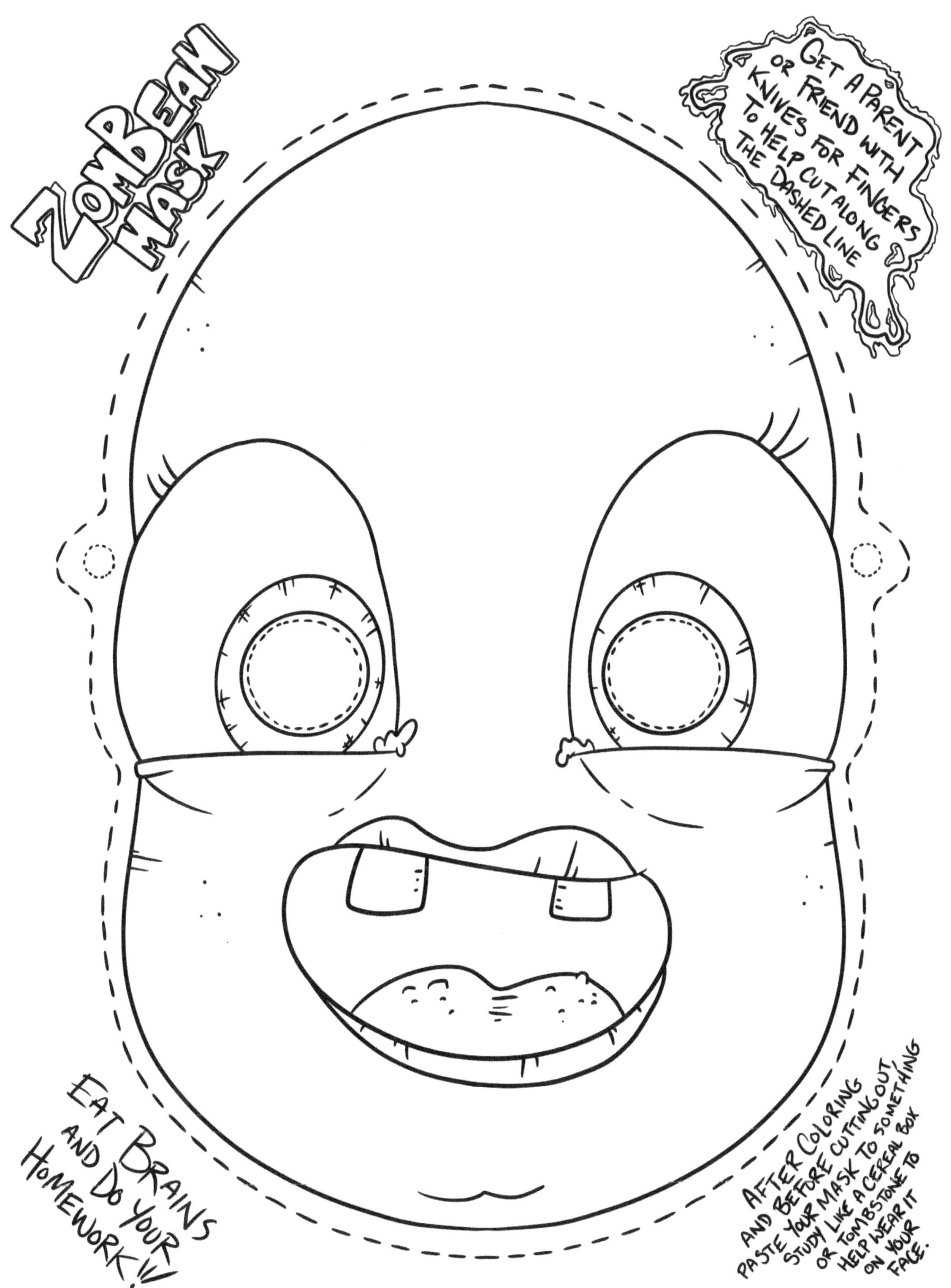

ZOMBEAN MASK
GET A PARENT OR FRIEND WITH KNIVES FOR FINGERS TO HELP CUT ALONG THE DASHED LINE
EAT BRAINS AND DO YOUR HOMEWORK!!
AFTER COLORING AND BEFORE CUTTING OUT PASTE YOUR MASK TO SOMETHING STUDY LIKE A CEREAL BOX OR TOMBSTONE TO HELP WEAR IT ON YOUR FACE.

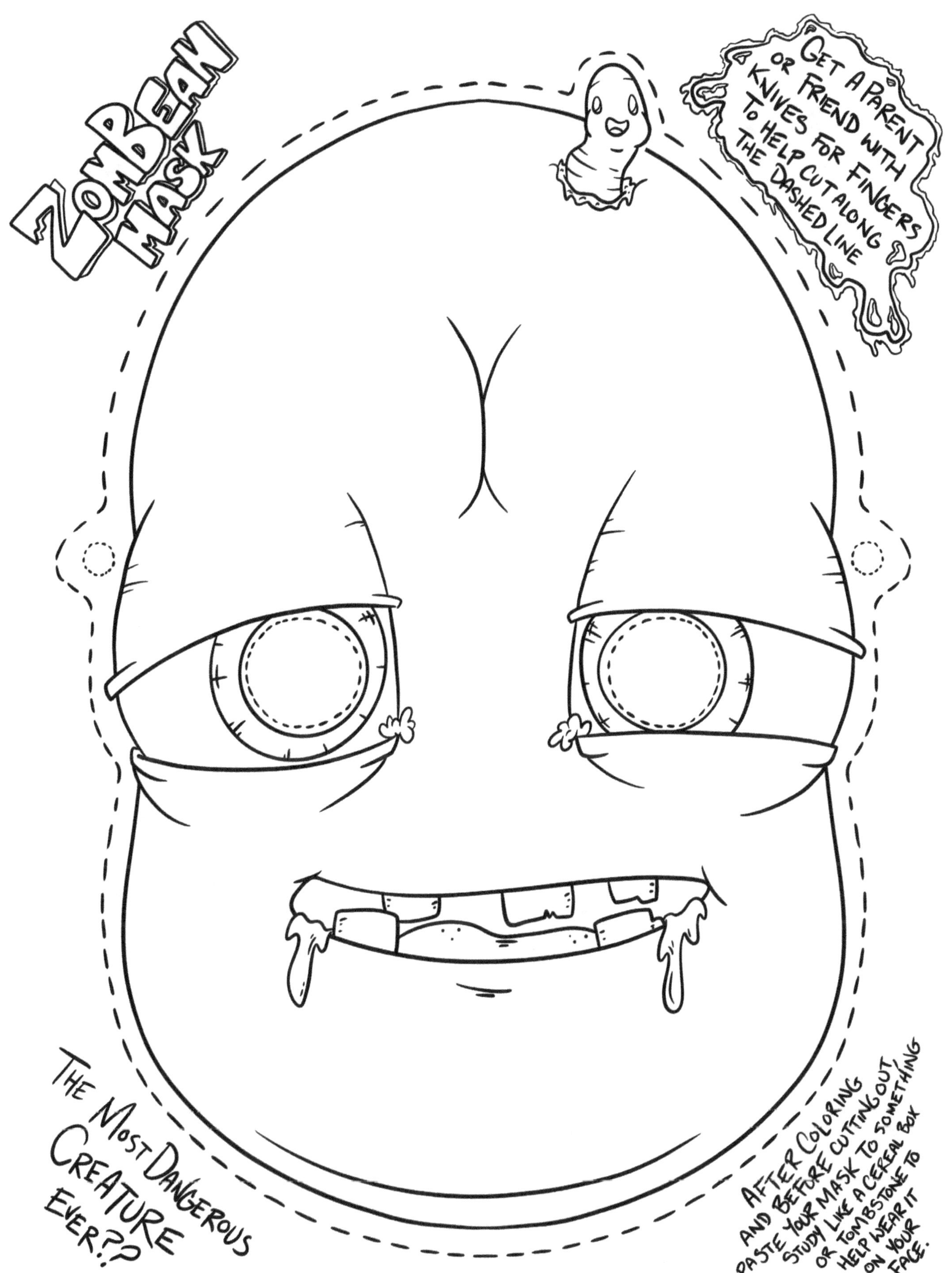

ZOMBEAN MASK
GET A PARENT OR FRIEND WITH KNIVES FOR FINGERS TO HELP CUT ALONG THE DASHED LINE
THE MOST DANGEROUS CREATURE EVER??
AFTER COLORING AND BEFORE CUTTING OUT PASTE YOUR MASK TO SOMETHING STUDY LIKE A CEREAL BOX OR TOMBSTONE TO HELP WEAR IT ON YOUR FACE.

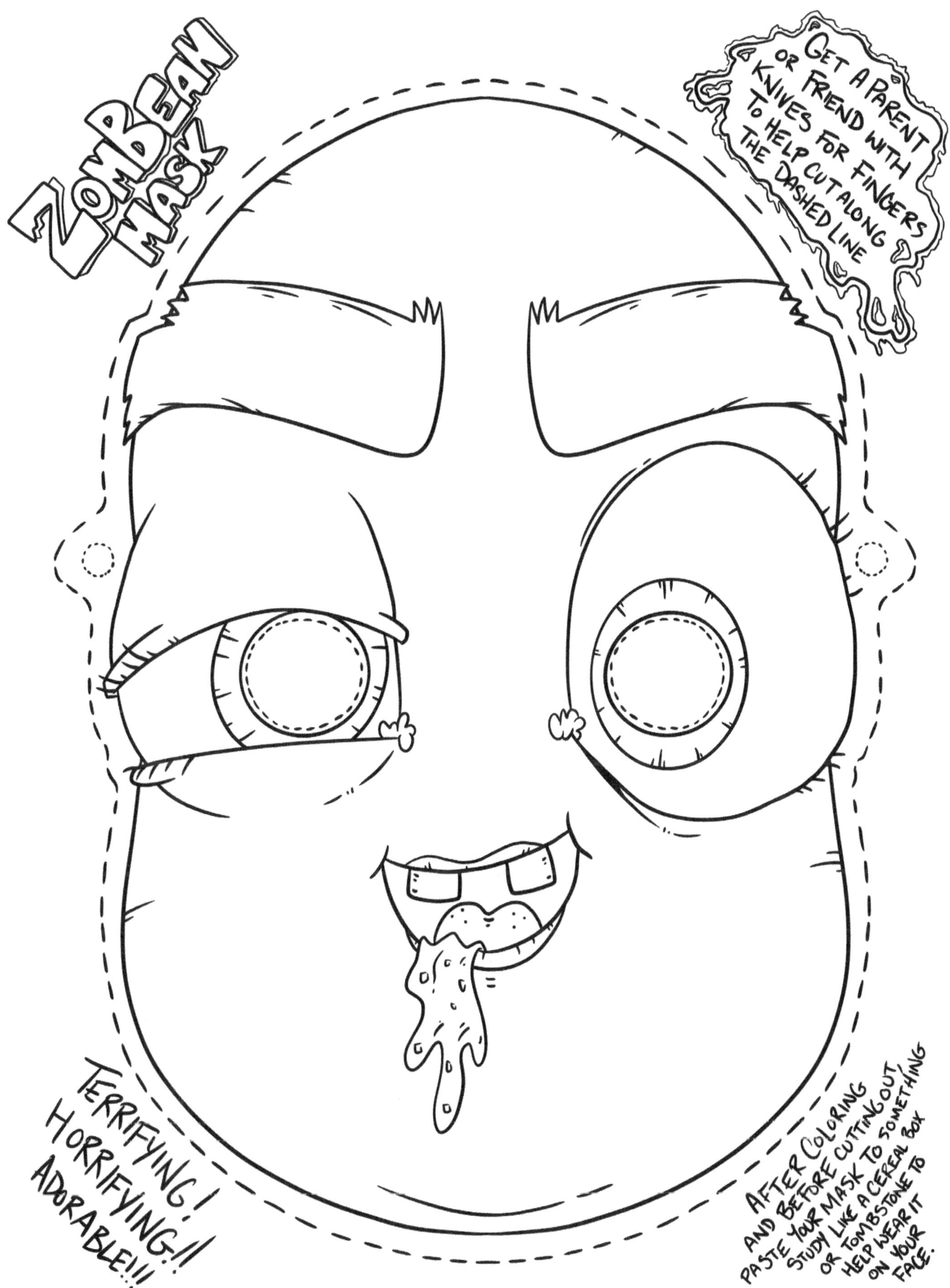

ZOMBEAN MASK
GET A PARENT OR FRIEND WITH KNIVES FOR FINGERS TO HELP CUT ALONG THE DASHED LINE
TERRIFYING! HORRIFYING!! ADORABLE!!!
AFTER COLORING AND BEFORE CUTTING OUT PASTE YOUR MASK TO SOMETHING STUDY LIKE A CEREAL BOX OR TOMBSTONE TO HELP WEAR IT ON YOUR FACE.

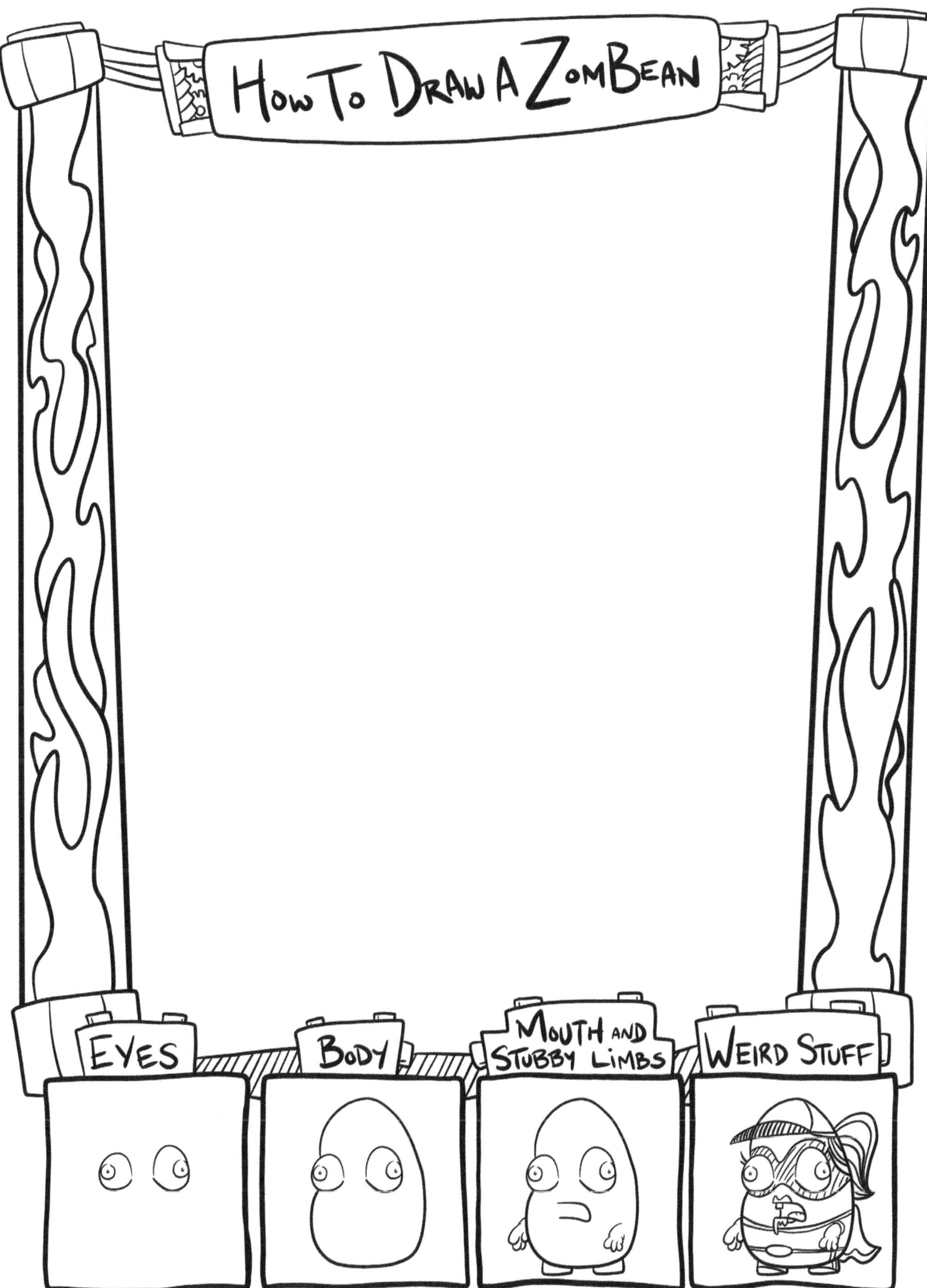

How To Draw A ZomBean
EYES
BODY
MOUTH AND STUBBY LIMBS
WEIRD STUFF

JOIN THE HORDE!

Get your monsters and more every month
when you sign up on Patreon

• Coloring Books • Stickers • Weird Stuff •
• ZOMBEANIFICATION •

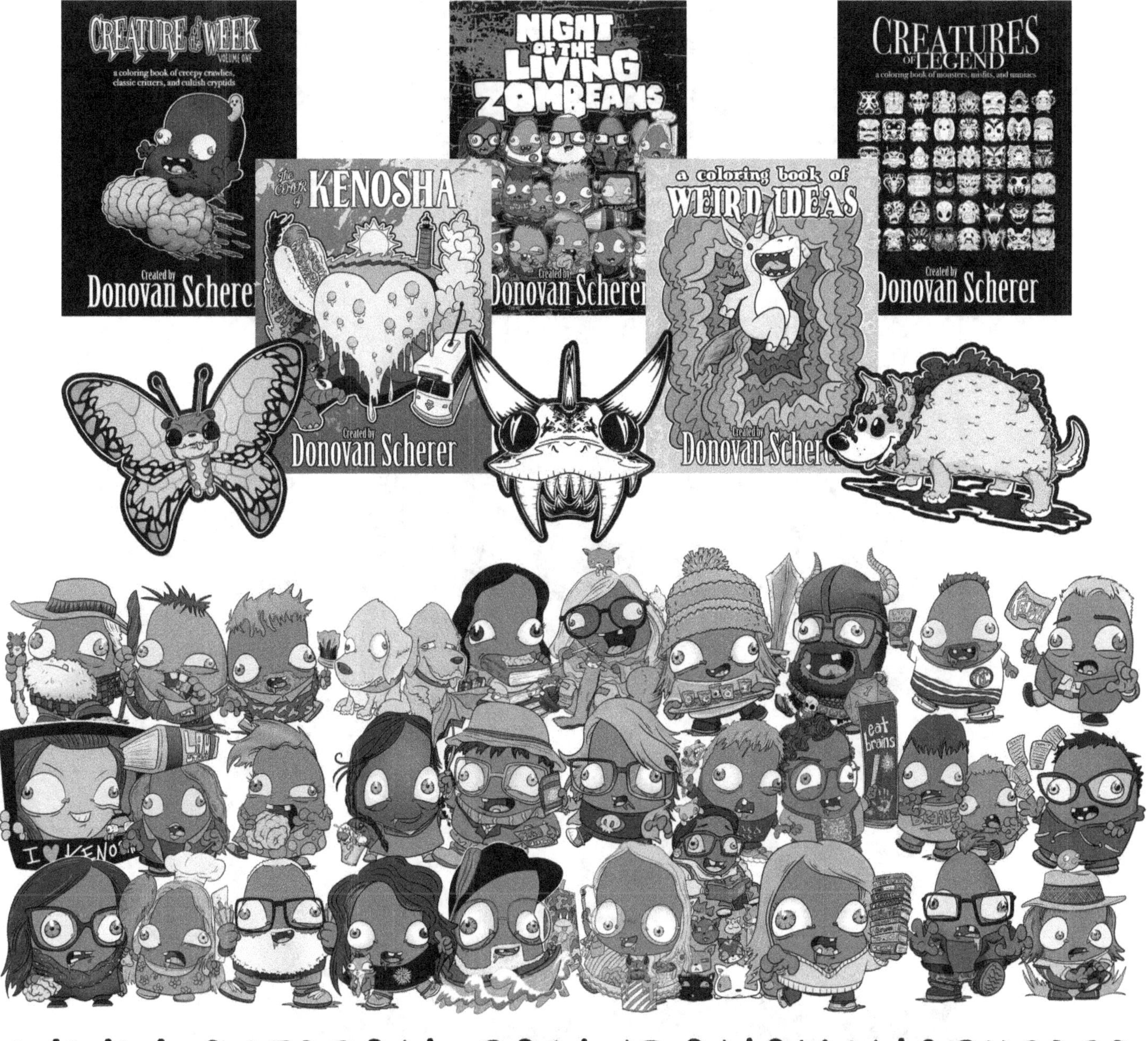

WWW.PATREON.COM/DONOVANSCHERER

VISIT STUDIO MOONFALL
ZAP IT!
PEW PEW!
VR
THROUGH THE MAGIC OF SCIENCE!
WWW.MOONFALL360.COM

WANT MORE TO COLOR?

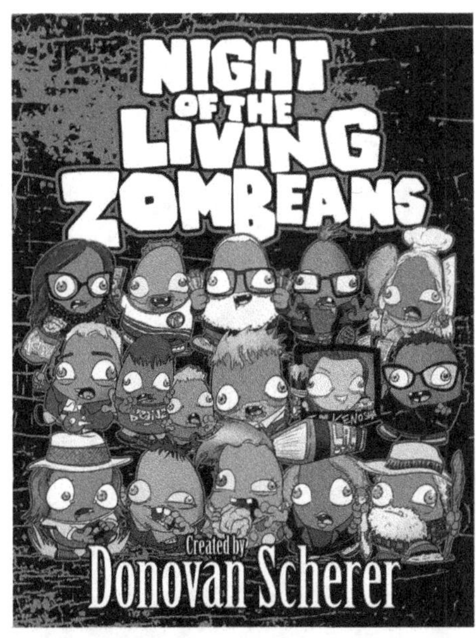

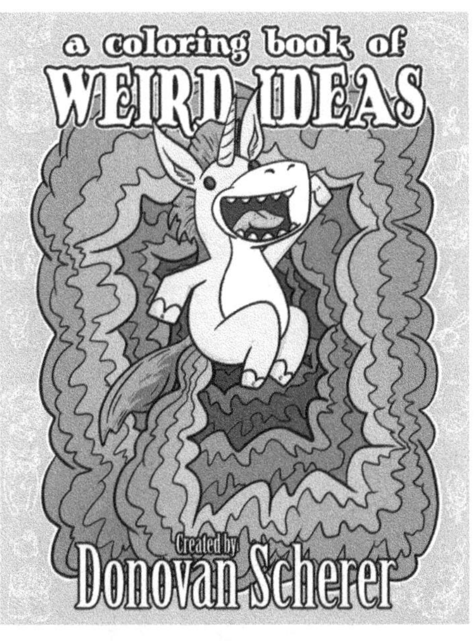

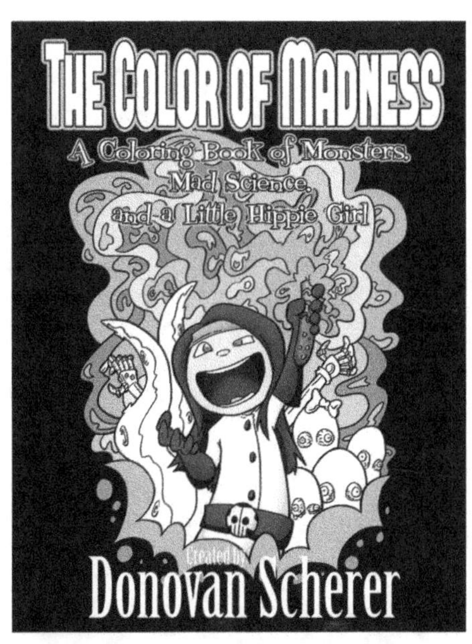

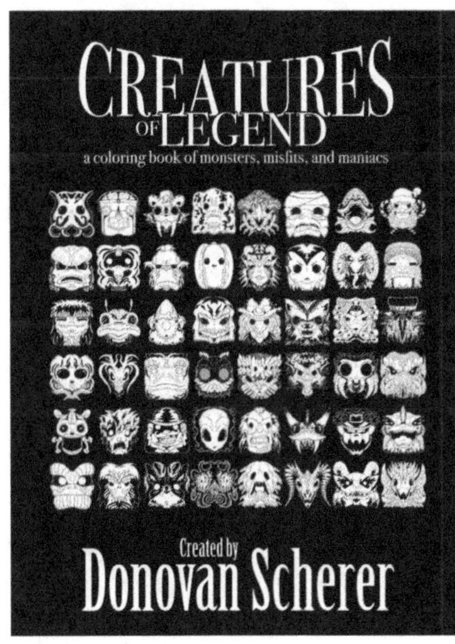

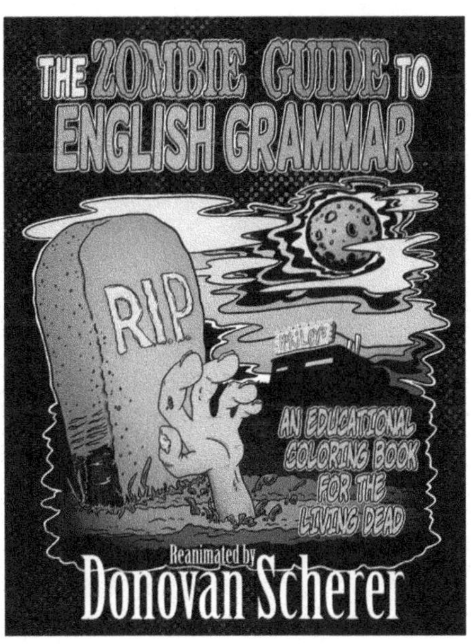

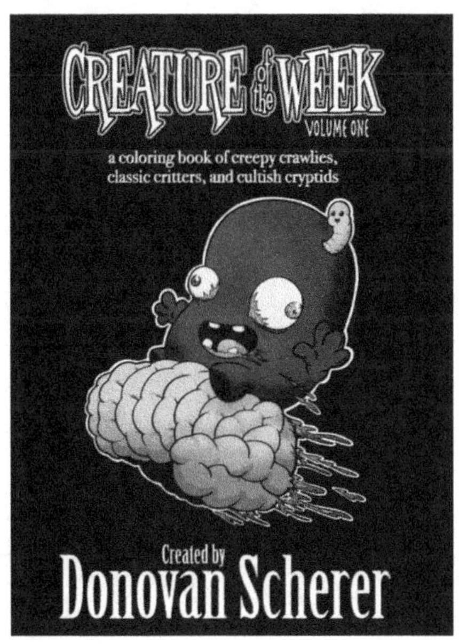

FIND YOUR NEXT COLORING BOOK AND MORE AT:

WWW.STUDIOMOONFALL.COM

www.ingramcontent.com/pod-product-compliance
Lightning Source LLC
Chambersburg PA
CBHW080350030726
47598CB00009B/2690